"I always speak the truth, even if I must lie to do so." Thus speaks Steven Peck's omniscient narrator Asmodeus. And he tells a hell of a story. *King Leere* is set in the near future in Utah mountains ravaged by climate change (the "koch catastrophe") and populated by Shakespearean Mormons, human-skinned goats, and battlebots. Asmodeus has been reading Nietzsche and Kierkegaard while adjusting to physical reality in Castle Valley, Utah. He's a savvy narrator who buries an encomium on a mule's hoof in a footnote so as not to impede the flow of his fantastic, apocalyptic, and exquisitely romantic narrative. Peck writes with scientific precision and poetic bravura (Leere himself speaks in blank verse!) and his marvelous cautionary tale leaves a reader richer on both counts.

—Scott Abbott
Professor of Integrated Studies,
Philosophy and Humanities
Utah Valley University

Semi-finalist for the Big Moose Prize for
unpublished novel manuscript contest at Black Lawrence Press

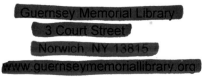

Is there room in a King Lear adaptation for battle droids? How about singing gene-modified porcupines and a demon narrator? Enter Peck's post-apocalyptic world populated by a land baron, his fractious progeny, and his herd of transgenic skin goats. In this futuristic dystopia, the real tragedy is that in a world warped by climate change, most of the characters are still fueled by consumerist greed, except for Delia and her lover, Ellie. But we all know what happens to the good guys. Or do we? Brilliant, imaginative, and wildly entertaining, Peck's adaptation of Shakespeare will appeal to hardcore bardolaters and those who wouldn't be caught dead in a theatre. This book is clever, funny, deeply thoughtful, and ambitious. A riot of a read.

—Dayna Kidd Patterson
Co-editor of *Dove Song: Heavenly Mother in Mormon Poetry*

As if part of the Hogarth Shakespeare's series where acclaimed novelists of today retell Shakespeare's works, Steven Peck brilliantly re-envisions Shakespeare's classic tragedy *King Lear*. Situated in the majestic landscape of the La Sal mountains in Utah, this is a dystopian, post-apocalyptic and ecologically resonant tale of possession, pride, misrecognition of true love and modesty, of blindness and insight. Peck skilfully entwines it with present-day issues of climactic change and humans' hurtling towards an apocalypse, thus turning this classic tale into a critique of the primacy of capital over human relationships and basic empathy.

Using humour, irony, and imbuing his novel with a sense of urgency over the fate of the planet, Peck has demon Asmodeus, formerly of Satan's infernal ranks, now reformed and living in La Sals, telling a "tragic tale framed in a not too distant future . . . a possible future. One that might be. Or might not be." Asmodeus is a self-proclaimed omniscient narrator, who nonetheless admits to the limits of his omniscience and who inserts interludes into the story where he waxes philosophical. He playfully expounds on Nietzsche and Kierkegaard, human nature and the possible outcomes of human flaws that are in the tragedy proper personified primarily by Lear and to an extent his offspring. The message however, is a more serious one, for it represents a lament for the planet and life on it, which hypothetically can be salvaged though not thorough human endeavour. Ultimately, the planet will survive once the humans are no longer there.

This is a novel that masterfully combines androids, genetically modified animals, retired infernal demons, legendary tragic characters (King Lear), a post-apocalyptic world with a vividly depicted, almost tangible local landscape of the La Sals, infused with popular culture references from *Buffy the Vampire Slayer* to *Star Trek the Next Generation*, but also Ancient Greek and Nordic mythology, Nietzsche and Kierkegaard, cowboys and the Wild West.

—Dr. Vanja Polić
Associate Professor, English Department
University of Zagreb, Croatia

In *The Tragedy of King Leere*, Steven Peck launches us into a future so haunting and dramatic and frightening, yet infinitely possible. That he makes this future seem so real and "normal" seemed impossible until I figured it out: he's been there, to the future. And fortunately for us, Steven Peck has come back from the future to tell us what he saw while we still have the chance to avoid it.

—Brooke Williams
Author of *Open Midnight*

BY COMMON CONSENT PRESS is a non-profit publisher dedicated to producing affordable, high-quality books that help define and shape the Latter-day Saint experience. BCC PRESS publishes books that address all aspects of Mormon life. Our mission includes finding manuscripts that will contribute to the lives of thoughtful Latter-day Saints, mentoring authors and nurturing projects to completion, and distributing important books to the Mormon audience at the lowest possible cost.

MR. STEVEN L.

PECK'S

THE TRAGEDY OF

KING LEERE,

GOATHERD OF

THE LA SALS.

WITH EXPERT COMMENTARY BY
MARY O'BRIEN

Published by By Common Consent Press
in Salt Lake City, Utah,

2019

For information contact
By Common Consent Press
4062 S. Evelyn Dr.
Salt Lake City, UT 84124-2250

Cover design: D Christian Harrison. Collage based on Thomas Sidney
    Cooper's *Highland Goats* (1850) and George Romney's (1734–1802)
    Lear in the Storm.
Book design: Andrew Heiss

www.bccpress.org

ISBN-13: 978-1-948218-01-6
ISBN-10: 1-948218-01-1

10 9 8 7 6 5 4 3 2 1

To my dad, who taught me to love the Earth

CONTENTS

ACKNOWLEDGEMENTS

Many people have contributed to this work. My writing group William Henry Morris, Scott Parkin, and the late Jonathan Langford, gave brilliant advice on early drafts that helped me feel like this novel was worth doing. Michael Austin and Jason Kerr were the first to read and critique Leere in its entirety and their early enthusiasm and belief in this project was essential in encouraging me to continue. Michael's critique was helpful beyond words, and Jason gave me advice and encouragement about working harder on Leere's iambic pentamterish voice. Beta readers included Jacek Adams, Brigham Daniels, Steve Evans, Ronan Head, Emily Grover, Kyle Monson, and Jaron Peck. Their work was helpful in improving and refining the book. Michael Austin and Andrew Heiss—my heroic editing team— were tireless and immensely patient as they worked to bring this work into something presentable. Christian Harrison's cover is magnificent and worthy of the great bard himself. Shannyn Thompson Walters did the copyediting without who this would be a wreck. Lastly, but not leastly, I'm grateful for my wife Lori and my wonderful kids who inspire me to new heights every day.

DRAMATIS PERSONÆ

KING LEERE	Landholder of the La Sals, Goatherd
HESTER GLOCK	Leere's girlfriend and common-law wife
DELIA LEERE	Leere's daughter
REGAN LEERE	Leere's son, Cornflower James' husband
NERIL LEERE	Leere's son, Edda's husband
ELLIE GLOCK	Hester's daughter
EDDA GLOCK	Hester's daughter, Neril's wife
CORNFLOWER JAMES	Daughter of Red "Doc" James, wife of Regan
FOOL	Botavita, Ex-Mormon Bishop
KENT	Knowledge Enabled Neural Tactical Banefinder BattleDredge
COWBOY BOB	Handy Ranch-Hand Bot
RED "DOC" JAMES	Owner of Polar Ridge and Dolorous Valley, Coloradan
READY JAMES	Ex-combat veteran of Chad / Somalia / Eritrea conflict, Coloradan
HAPPY ORANGE INDUSTRIES	Builder of fine weapons

ACT I

CASTLE VALLEY NEAR MOAB, UTAH

ASMODEUS' REFLECTIONS

Cloudy days in late autumn are scarce in this thirsty part of the world. The thick gray canopy seems to lift rather than oppress in its promise of one of those rare after-monsoon season rains. As the advancing evening slides into the darkening canyon, the unfolding gloaming brings a muted quiet as varying shades of red and black disclose a new canyon to my senses. One that, although I see daily, is one I've never seen before. I think you know what I mean—every cloud, each angle of the sun, an individual act of light precipitation, all bring me to a place I've never been before, conditioned on a mood of temperature, or the voice of a particular bird, or even what humor I find within myself. All of these things flavor which colors and hues I see. So this unfolding landscape is born anew at this very moment, and, although, bearing a close family resemblance to the other canyons I observe here daily, it is nevertheless a novel thing in the world if only from my perspective.

But you know all this. Such observations on "perspective" border on cliché. They've been noted a thousand times. You've seen it done again and again from Monet's Rouen Cathedral series to Gilda Trillim's Appleseed Paintings. Change the light, change the reality. Move a little to the left and a new world is created. Let a butterfly flit by in the foreground and the landscape is remade.

Whatever. I revel in cliché these days. I want to bask in the repeatable. I want to dwell among the ordinary: barbwire, backroads, a leaky faucet, a rusty wheelbarrow by white chickens and all that. I've spent my life directing beings toward emptiness and doom. Let me now enjoy a sunset on the steep cliffs about me and change the world by tilting my head. Leave me to my clichés. I'm enjoying them immensely.

As the sun sets behind the sheltering red rock mothering this ancient valley, I notice that it is now starting to sprinkle. The moisture leaves dark patches of wet dirt—except where the ground is sheltered by one of the abundant sagebrushes scattered here and there on the sandy, ochre soil. Red silt, like the protective walls that nurture and contain us, is a constant companion in canyon country. The clouds from the east are especially dark suggesting that more rain might at any time find its way to this remote hideaway. I even fancy I see a few flashes of lightning portending a more impressive downpour.

The window of my trailer home unveils a rather desolate view. A broken fence. A half-buried, rusting disk plow. A modest pile of ancient discarded truck tires. There, to the left of my driveway, are the remnants of a corral, whose rotting planks have lost both the fashion of their function, and the substance of their structure, yet even so, hint at forgotten bovine purposes. The rough planks of remnant wood have become infused with cracking, dry rot, and are blessed with that dull gray aspect of weathered lumber no longer of any use to humans.

This is my home. I have my books, my computer, and enough money, leisure, and inclination, to give in to a desire to step back and tell you a tale. It is about possible future events that will transpire in the mountains that grace my view to the Southeast. I haven't lived here long, yet this valley is a convenient launching point for my story.

Castle Valley is about twenty miles up the Colorado River from Moab, Utah and has been infested mainly with artists, ranchers, and those poor enough or rich enough to live in such isolation. It has always been so. But as the warming and drying continues, the crowd has thinned. Much to my contentment. For the heat does not bother me (and no jokes, please, about it being because I am adapted to the fires of Hell, such mythologies I despise even in humor).

Where do I fit in such a taxonomy? Where indeed. I hesitate to delve too deeply into my story lest I detract from the real purpose I put ink to paper (as it were, I think we need a new expression which is more modern than "ink to paper" yet captures the pleasure in writing that "fingers to keyboard" does not). But I cannot leave you too ignorant, or none of this will make sense.

First on the list of facts that I must disclose is that I am an omniscient narrator by avocation. A daemon by trade. Call me Asmodeus (even though I am not the *Asmodeus of Biblical fame, I once had aspirations to be like him and held him as a personal hero, and so early in my career took his name). To look at me in corporeal form no doubt you would think me fiercely ugly, but I can resemble humans enough to fall within the range of variation deemed possible, but barely—enough humanness to carefully walk among you without receiving too wrenching a shudder. As such, I can typically* mingle in human company just long enough to secure those things I deem necessary for my entertainment and survival.

In human form, you would think my nose absurdly long and crooked—bending downward at an unfortunate angle. My face is equipped with a prominent chin that combined with my nose gives me a rhinoceros beetle aspect in profile—a visage that might feel more at home in a Mervyn Peake sketch. This look is present only when I become entirely infested with matter, which ability is a story in itself, but one I will not bore you with now. Suffice it to say I have become completely enamored with being embodied. Not in the ordinary sense that one achieves in possession, say, but in the fullness of physical existence. I can take other metaphysical forms, but my preference is to the material. The bodily embrace of space and time. However, noncorporeal forms allow me to slip and slide into the consciousness of others, whether instantiated in animal, vegetable, or mineral. So I use it as I must for my narrations. A useful talent for one of my employ, or former employment, I should say. Perhaps some explanation of that is warranted.

You must find it odd to find me here deep in the Canyonlands of Southern Utah. Would you not expect a daemon, such as myself, to be more likely found strolling down the Kärtner-Ring Strasse in Vienna? Or the Boulevard Saint-Michel in Paris? Somewhere surely more conducive to culture? (Generally, the daemons' reputation for being highly cultured is not undeserved and rarely overstated). But the weather here suits my new existential leanings quite nicely. Thank you very much. You see, I no longer serve Satan, nor fight against the Almighty One. I have refused to play the part of either. Neither engaging in endless skirmishes with the One's incipient angels and their sordid attempts to sort each other into some kind of hierarchy (a temptation that seems to infect both sides of the battle, but seems worse among the angelic hosts). Nor do I brawl with the infernal legions diabolically arrayed like tin soldiers on a toy store shelf. No. I've separated myself from the war entirely. That is why I find I have some leisure on my hands. Of course, everyone cries foul, "If you are not with us you are against us." Both obsessed sides denounce me, trying to edge me back into the fray. But I'm done. Let the forces of good and evil battle it out among themselves. Perhaps when they've worn themselves out in eternal bickering, truly the meek will inherit the Earth, or what's left of it.

Oddly, it was Nietzsche who freed me. His move to go beyond these senseless categories of good and evil was brilliant. For three years I read everything he wrote, sometimes reading the same book over and over. Also Sprach Zarathustra was my favorite, even so, it was Zur Genealogie der Moral that awakened the motivation to escape the conflict. After, I looked at the great war between good and evil, with its endless suffering, pointless victories, failures and faints, and thought to myself that the time had come to step aside and content myself with using my freedom to concentrate on the real task of any life—to become an Überdaemon, in the Nietzschean sense, rather than the Buffy the Vampire Slayer variety—and to focus my efforts on becoming something more than my programming (You will no doubt note the reference to Data from Star Trek the Next Generation). So my task became to forget everyone's agenda, even the One's and Satan's and work on those values and virtues that I find inherent in being an existing individual (yes, I have since read Kierkegaard).

And so, finding myself unemployed, I became an omniscient narrator. A more humble occupation but one that suits my *newfound existential predilections. And I am a trustworthy one, for I always speak the truth, even if I must lie to do so.*

So here I sit at a desk in a Brentwood trailer in the middle of nowhere. I have not tried to tempt my neighbors to some absurd evil, nor have I sought their salvation, nor even their friendship. (I am not yet ready to explore Buber's I and Thou, or Levinas' "Other," as they are tainted by the endless warring factions of the "great battle"). I ignore these human neighbors, and they ignore me. What contentment I've found lies in that arrangement.

But to the tragic tale framed in a not too distant future. However future is a dicey thing, conditioned on probabilities, rather than necessities. So I must be careful in the use of my language (Carnap the great positivist philosopher of the Vienna Circle would be so proud). This is a possible future. One that might be. Or might not be. You will decide I suppose. By "you" of course I mean you of your race. Humans as you call yourself. Time means nothing to me. Space means little. However, even given that power, I do still enjoy a quiet evening by a fire reading.

Enough of my reminiscences. To the tragic tale at hand. To understand what let me introduce the most important member of our troupe, Leere, Goatherd King of the La Sals. The rest will follow in due course, but he is the anti-hero in this anti-play, and so some clarity as to his nature and history must begin this venture.

DESCRIBING LEERE THE KING

To describe the old man's face one must reference his demeanor. Demeanor through and through, up and down, high and low, in and out, in fact out of any number of his dimensional attributes it is demeanor that carries the day. Of some men you might say, "he is of thick-lips" or "weak in the chin," of another perhaps, "delicate" or "firm of jaw," or "heavily browed, with peering eyes that communicated something porcine and sinister" for example. On ordinary faces, each feature might be described singly, with each nuance of aspect considered in turn, in hopes that in the summation of each trait, some sense of countenance might be illustrated. But of the King, as he was called, one could only bring all his features together at once and reference them in total, as I have said—his demeanor. I suspect if you saw him riding his bay mule up on Taylor's Flat in the La Sals, you might say to your companion, "Did you see that cowboy's demeanor?" For it would stand out entirely, even from below the brim of his white felt hat. Yes, his face was all demeanor through and through. His visage was of such demeanoresque purity that it suggested an ideal form of a type that some ancient Greek philosopher cataloging the inhabitants of an ethereal realm might list: truth, beauty, goodness, demeanor.

It was not always so. As a young man you certainly would not have called him handsome, but neither was he an eyesore. He was a quick-witted lad, able and willing to take such dares as he thought he could win, but he could confidently and without hesitation brush off those that seemed imprudent or rash or those likely to end poorly—those that in the end might suggest a foolishness, he was reluctant to countenance. Back then he seemed of an ordinary sort. Not one you would pick out for either glory or disaster. So when he left Moab to seek his fortune, his friends all wished him well and forgot all about him.

Years later he returned as rich as Croesus. No one knows how he came upon his wealth. Rumors floated thick, mostly conveying some suspicion of dirty dealing. Some said he made it in cocaine from Columbia. Others that he opened a porn studio in LA. A few claimed he found a cache of treasure during the war on one of the Islands of Southeast Asia. One rumor held that he went to Russia and landed a position as riding instructor with a royal princess from the Russian Mafia and as in a fairytale they had fallen in love and the boss of that crime family paid a fortune for him to abandon his suit (the question of why he was not just summarily killed outright suggests this story likely a myth). But no one knew, and of his money he would say nothing, or if he ever did tell trusted friends, they were faithful to whatever oaths of secrecy they were made to swear.

He bought the mountain. He bought out the Wixoms. He bought out the Baniffs. From Taylor Flats to Pack Creek he owned whatever land was buyable in the La Sals, which after the infamous Privatization Act just before the war which, of course, destroyed the concept of public land, was all of it. To those reluctant to sell, he snatched up water and mineral and grazing rights all around them, and left them with a whole lot of nothing until they saw it the better part of folly to resist, and handed him over their deeds.

It was worthless land anyway, this was right after the drought, the war, and the great schism. Pick your poison from that era. You know the ones I mean. First, the drought that razed the West and devoured its forests. The one that emptied the aquifers and stole the winter snow and replaced it with hard summer rains that uprooted rather than sated the soil. The one that sent the spurge and contrary cheat grasses and medusahead wildrye up the flanks of the mountains replacing what green forage used to flourish with hard husked plants and twisted dry barked sage that grow when the landscape goes grim and dry and mocks the beasts that try to eat them. The drought that brought insect pests and fungal diseases to the trees of the forest. With the drought, came the civil war. The water and *drainage rights pitted the Southwest against California, the floods of the Missouri pitted the Midwest against the South, and soon ideologues reigned, and the US broke apart. This followed war with other countries, and so the world itself raged. But this tale is not of those things. Still, these terrors played to the King's advantage and he emerged as one of the economic powers in the Western States Alliance—the western states sans California. The effects of these resource wars included displaced peoples, destabilized economies— as ever money flowed to arrange and rearrange the world, making some rich and destroying others. However, to dwell on these things would be to lose altogether the tale that needs telling—a tiny microcosm in a play of much higher and more deadly stakes. All you need to know is that things settled down, new borders were drawn, new entities emerged, and some soldiers came home and some did not. But the landscape both socially and politically had changed. Although not changed as drastically as the world's ecosystems. Not even close.*

Leere, raised Mormon, soon found himself outside its aegis in all its manifestations—and there were many.† But the King was a man who knew how to exploit almost anything for gain. He knew what to do, when others bowed their heads in despair. He would work this land. He would wring from it what would be wrung.

---

† Here in what used to be called Utah, the single Mormon Church had fractured into several groups. Only three need mentioning as they bear on this story: (1) The great institutional church once centered in Salt Lake City moved to Independence, Missouri to usher in the Millennium for which they are still waiting, this is still the largest and richest denomination of the former entity; (2) the Church of Jesus Christ of Every-day Agapests (EDAs) a group that focused on love, diversity, and equality—still calling themselves Mormon they make up most of the former Western Alliances and European members; (3) The FLDS, the polygamists. Still active but isolationist in the extreme.

At first, he bought up some heat tolerant zebu cattle herds from the Sahel of Africa and set the drought hardy beasts upon the La Sals. He traded out sheep for a breed of large African goats. Cheatgrass was a treat compared to whatever Sahel thorns these livestock were bred to subsist on and they flourished. By then the deer and elk and other wild ungulates had been driven north and into the Canadian Rockies.

However, the warming continued apace, and soon even the African goats could not keep up with the drying land and the warming air. The Hadley cells that drive the earth's winds and rains stretched outward as some models predicted, and the great Sonoran Desert slithered northward toward Albuquerque, New Mexico.

But Leere was not one to let the drying earth have its way. He replaced the beasts with new human-forged animals that could withstand the unnatural rigors of the new regime. And he again flourished. These transgenic animals were created, under his specifications, especially for this land and its climatic terrors. Intelligently designed for both the La Sals and the King's purposes.

He grew richer, and as he did, his face gained the arroyoed demeanor for which he was famous. It was a dry and heartless face like the land. It grew merciless. And his eyes became dry and jaundiced, filled with resentment—bitter and narrow. Full of suspicions he became. His gaze roamed this way and that. And with the fear that all around were creatures shrewd and fierce, willing to take what moisture had been hoarded for you and yours. His thin hair grew wiry, colored grey-blue like the leaves of a sage. And his lips were split and parched like the cracked, desiccated mud long dried from a cruel monsoon rain. And if allowed, I could start a thousand sentences with "Ands." For there are not enough "ands" to describe this pitiable and empty and complex man. Nor raise a hope of excavating his demeanor.

As this theatric tragedy begins, he is old and his once sharp mind is not now what it once was. Like a prophet-king of old, it was time to divide his land among his offspring and give them their inheritance. This is Leere. Goatherd King of the La Sals.

—*Asmodeus*

ACT II

LEERE'S RANCH HOUSE
IN THE LA SALS

SCENE I: KENT IS UNPACKED

The hard gray plastic crate measures $7' \times 3' \times 3'$ and rests on two pine sawhorses placed in the Great Room of Leere's massive log cabin mansion. The room is lavishly decorated with rustic driftwood furniture, Navaho rugs, and a large bear hide he bought off a rancher's son who claimed it had actually been from a bear that lived in the La Sals (isotopic analysis suggested an origin in Alaska). Mounted above a massive fireplace is a taxidermist's vision of a moose's head, with large expansive antlers spread wide in a welcoming gesture. Above him in the rafters are numerous sun-bleached mule deer and elk antlers gathered from the ground after the die off—the "Devastation" during the terrible drought. These are the product of his frequent excursions through his property. The King still gets a thrill when he finds one of these remnants of the previous generation. Antlers mean these mountains once teemed with life, just as they do now with his goats. And as they always will, for what nature throws at humans, humans can respond to with their own kind of fierce tenacity—or so Leere held. Their own kind of hostile takeover of what remains, as he often claimed. Those trophies he collected, nestled in the crossbeams are of various sizes and all mounted securely on the struts, gave him a sense of totem power over the land, as if by hoarding what once could not stand up to nature's cruelties, he can keep these animal's failure to survive from creeping into his holdings. He especially likes the big racks, and he was good at finding them. When the kids were little he would often take them antler hunting, and when they found one, it was always an event, celebrated with gunfire, hoots and hollers, and a strange joyous dance. Several of the antlers hanging above him are attached to specific memories. Most of them precious.

A hush of air is detectable from the solar powered air conditioning system that cools the log house to a comfortable 72 degrees from the 106 outside. Cowboy Bob, a "Handy Ranch Hand s4" (a model several years old) lies dead in one corner, his legs akimbo, twisted in unnatural ways. It languishes where his body was thrown two days ago, after being shot while mending fences. It was the James family, of that the King is sure.

Leere looks around his home—the center place for his Kingdom. It stretches from the Dolores River to the Colorado, completely enclosing the Earth's greatest laccoliths, the La Sal mountains which rise both South and East of his home.

He is alone today. He wants it that way. His oldest son Regan and his wife Cornflower James, have gone down to Moab to shop. His son, Neril and his daughter in law Edda (the daughter of his own common-law wife Hester) have taken the goat cart for a ride up Beef Basin. Delia, his youngest daughter, was likely off to Park City with her friend, Ellie, his wife's other daughter—who knows what those two were up to. She of course is coming home this weekend for the big "reading" and he will be glad to see her. She has been gone nearly two months and he misses her smile. She is the apple of his eye as everyone knows it.

But right now, he is not thinking about his kids. Now we find him walking around the large case smiling, running his hand along the hard shiny, gray plastic casing that protects its precious, and very, very expensive, and hard to obtain contents. His hand hovers over the locking mechanism that has kept the treasure secure on its journey from Brazil. The surface of the plastic is cold to the touch. Its lovely smoothness and shine communicate efficiency and power.

It is time.

He takes out a DepCon dedicated pad that has come with the case, he activates it with his neural implant and presses the power button on the side. He looks wide-eyed into the blank screen. A pleasant voice says,

Retinal scan complete please say the passphrase.

"The glorious La Sal Mountains are the
most beautiful place on Earth and they are
mine and I am them. Amen and amen."

Passphrase confirmed. Voice pattern match confirmed. Please place your finger on the DNA sampling mechanism.

A small button on the bottom with a tiny hole out of which the sampling pin will protrude marks the place. He puts his finger over the button.

Fingerprint confirmed.

There had been a barely noticeable prick to his finger.

> DNA match confirmed. Testing blood for presence of unusual metabolic activity and searching for possible coercive drugs . . . Living being confirmed.
>
> Acting without pharmaceutical coercion confirmed.

It is done. It is his body. He is alive and there are no drugs influencing his opening the case. He wondered how many dead bodies had been used to open such things as this before they took such measures to ensure identity.

The screen fires to life.

> Good Morning Mr. Leere. Welcome to your new military grade Knowledge Enabled Neural Tactical Banefinder BattleDredge (KENT_BBD). This is Happy Orange Industries' (HOI's) most advanced tactical sentient android . . .

"Skip introduction," the King said.

> Skipping introduction.
>
> Mr. Leere would you like to activate your new android?

"Activate."

The locking mechanism releases its catch and the lid and the sides of the case begin to fold up and dissolve. Within minutes, standing between the sawhorses is a BattleDredge. Six feet tall, it stands upon thin black skeletal legs. Its torso is encased in black titanium-carbon alloy, which the promotional literature claims is impervious to anti-tank projectiles. Its round head has a corona of silver about six inches thick, and that acts as ears, eyes, and nose. Its top two forearms end with large, seven-fingered, and two-thumbed hands, its bottom two are weapons. When it bends its elbows of weaponized appendages, one can see the hollow barrels of the .50 cal., exploding sabot round on the left arm and the 7.62 laser guided sniper rifle on the right. Its full tool kit includes multiple grenades, two anti-tank missiles, a Gatling gun that fires high-velocity carbon bullets that it manufactures out of the CO_2 in the air and various other light armor weapons. It looks intimidating and dangerous. With a high capacity backpack attached, its arsenal expands significantly. This is highly illegal of course, owning a military-grade weapon like this could mean prison time if people spread the news too broadly. And if he were less rich. But he is the King. He got what he wanted. Greater Brazil does not care who bought weapons as long as the money is good. And his is.

What do we make of this? This purchase of a weapon owned by only a few of the more powerful states on this planet that appears so anxiously to be sliding into senescence? I fear that the planet's demise might stand as a metaphor for Leere's own dementia. It has been noticed by his sons. And perhaps by his daughter as well. And who will give heed to a man in the throws of dementia? Who will acknowledge that his faculties are failing and that all he says should be taken with not only a grain of salt, but with perhaps a sea of it? It will not be those who can gain by it. Oh no. Those whose power rests on his will keep him propped like a puppet and let him say his lines with Shakespearian pathos. Who is to gain o' reader from his infirmity? That we will see. In what happens next!

— *Asmodeus*

He commands the sizeable golem to move outside and puts it through its paces in non-sentient mode. It reminds the old man of playing video games when he was a youngster. It has been a long time. What fun!

The beast moves with such silence and grace! He has it run up the steep hill that rises behind the house, and it sprints with such smooth comportment as to take his breath away. It climbs under his command to the top of a large ponderosa pine from which it leaps to the ground. It lands like a cat with only minimal noise. He launches it into the air with its Tenndyl engines and it flies above dry steppe like a witch on a broomstick, diving, and then rising to meet the clouds.

He brings it down and moves it back into the house. Such a grin he wears! This little device will indeed take care of the problems with the Jameses.

"Set up targeting instructions now, please."

Ready.

"All humans will never targeted be."

No humans. Confirmed.

"No goats, variety JLH3."

No goats of variety JLH3. Confirmed.

"The parameters of engagement are
Clear said. All equines, camels, ATVs,
Any vehicle mechanical, may
Fired on be, to a mission secure."

Clarification. To cause repairable damage, irreparable damage, or to obliterate beyond using any component parts?

"Irreparable damage."

Irreparable damage confirmed. Should passengers of such vehicles be damaged?

"No humans."

Human passengers unharmed. Confirmed.

"If being fired upon any kind
of weapon fell may targeted, again hear,
no humankind may be fired upon.

Confirmed weapons may be disabled. No part of a human may be damaged.

"Correct."

"Continuing desired war target
Specification. Human structures may
Be targeted only under my proved
And confirmed authorized active command."

Structures targeted only under Mr. Leere's direct command.

"All predators, coyotes, wolves, cougars, dogs,
and high eagles target at will freely.

Clarification, Those species, except coyotes, are protected under the Protectorate of the Western Alliance endangered species act, please confirm action and initiate local law override.

"Override all laws."

Confirmed all laws overridden.
Confirmed all predatory animals may be killed.

"Upload file, 'Family Portraits.' Any of
Humans so scanned may be helped at any time.
If they are in danger, all previous
Commands to lower priority fall."

Clarification. Including commands not to fire on
humans?

"If such members of given 'Family
Portraits' so request or their lives found in
Clear, present danger of death or hurt, yes."

Protection of "Family Portraits" confirmed.

The programming goes on for hours. After direct pro-gramming, the setup protocols propose another hour of possible scenarios to allow its neural net to weight properly its basic ethical subroutines. These are constructed along the lines of, "Suppose Family Member Regan is being attacked by sen-tient enemy drone fire, but Family Member Hester requests help to rescue grandchildren in a foundering boat, the prob-ability of Regan being killed by the drone is 0.873, while the probability of the boat capsizing is 0.45 but both children will be lost if it capsizes . . .

The King, however, is patient with the learning program. This is not something you want to get wrong. Or do sloppily. These could be matters of life and death. Getting these things right was what made the difference between feeling secure at night, and gross uncertainties this thing might engender.

The last thing he does is upload the Ranch Boundary Map.

"Actions take place only within given
Boundaries marked in the RBM file."

Displaying areas of engagement map with area of engagement highlighted. Is this the area of active hostilities?

"Yes."

Areas of engagement confirmed.

Mr. Leere. The unit's sentient capabilities are now ready to be uploaded. Please listen to the following warning which you may not skip. Your weapon's sentient capabilities range from fully deterministic rule following, to high levels of independent learning and engagement. The higher levels of sentience allow teleodynamic processes to emerge in its Mind (Registered Trademark). We recommend that these processes be allowed to run no longer than 48 hours. Studies have shown that if allowed to run longer, the unit has a small risk of becoming unstable. If your missions last longer, it is recommended that a remote reboot be performed after every 24 hours, currently your unit is set to do this operation automatically. It takes 3.5 seconds for the reboot and we recommend it be overridden when the unit is engaged in combat. Would you like to keep these restrictions in place?

"Remove restrictions."

Confirmed: Restrictions removed.

"In the event of catastrophic instability, your unit is equipped with a 0.3m Buckminster Fuller explosive next to the neural processing unit found in your unit's abdominal cavity. This may not be removed and if tampered with it will set off the device. It

will also be detonated if the preprogrammed ethical
subroutines are tampered with, see enclosed files to
understand the nature and purpose of these ethical
routines. You are also reminded that according to the
licensing agreement with Happy Orange Industries this
unit may be disabled by our prerogative at any time.
It should be noted that Happy Orange Industries takes
no sides in conflicts and reserves this right only for
its own protection and the protection of its interests. Please refer to the licensing agreement. Do you
agree to everything found within that document?

"I agree."

Are you ready to set up the personality profile?

"Yes. High fidelity to my person.
Reward mission-objective success with
A blessed ecstasy level reward.
Mission failure pain level set at six.
Scale linearly between these extremes for
Completion partial. Full web download for
Informational access, with ample
Creativity and innovation
On high set. Voice and gender attributes
<uummm> male. Human interface natural and
Friendly for non-military or child
Encounters. Mission loyalty? Always
High! Let anger levels be ever found
Situationally normal.

"Setting up personality profile."

"Personality profile integration complete. Your KENT_BDD is ready for use."

The great being of destruction does not look any different. It stands there silent and motionless. No lights blink indicating that it is alive as seen in the old 2D movies.

"Hello, Kent."

"Hello Mr. Leere," it said in a pleasant clear natural voice.

"Mr. Leere. I am detecting a damaged HOI 'Handy Ranch Hand s4' approximately 11 meters from me. I am equipped to repair all HOI androids if you have the universal repair kit—which I detect you do. Would you like me to initiate repairs?"

"Yes."

The battle dredge goes over to a large tool box about a fourth of the size of the crate the BattleDredge came in and quickly gatheres several items and tools into a smaller satchel. It quickly moves to the damaged cowhand lying next to the wall—still dressed in its work clothes: jeans, and an ensemble of cowboy shirt, boots, and hat.

"I see that it has been shot with a .306 round to the main transference junction causing a loss of sentience. I'll now repair it."

Its work is lightning fast, its handling of the tools proficient and exact. In less than a minute the battle dredge picks up the control pad laying next to the wounded android and turns it on.

"This model will take 87 seconds to power up."

It walks over and replaces the tools it used.

The King watches as the ranch hand returns to sentience. After rebooting the silly thing sits up looks at the BattleDredge, then looks at Leere and nodding toward the weapon says, "Who the Hell is this bandito?"

"Cowboy Bob. Meet Kent, a new BattleDredge," the aged goat King says.

Cowboy Bob looks up at the KENT BattleDredge, "Damn and Tarnation where in the Hell did this monstrosity come from? This hunk of baling wire is gonna be more worthless than a solar panel in a silver mine—it ain't like we are at war."

Cowboy Bob moves to give the weapon a playful punch on the shoulder, but the mechanical man catches his fist and holds it still.

"Let go of me you son of a bitching ham radio that was fathered by a dime store mannequin."

"Release the Handy Ranch Hand now good Kent," the King says smiling,

"I forgot to mention he is also
Under my fair and gifted protection.

"Damn toot'n I am, you lumbering batch of gru-steel and tumbleweed inspired neural circuits—I'm under this here King's protection so save that on yer hard drive somewhere."

"Registered," says the KENT.

"Reggggissstered," mocks Cowboy Bob.

"That's enough Bob. Don't you have work to do?"

"I reckon so, yer Majesty, but if yer Grace will indulge me in ask'n 'bout a curiosity fer yer humble servant that's got me right flummoxed."

"What?" the King answers impatiently.

"Why I just wanted to get a notion what sort of asshole would gun down a Handy Ranch Hand. I mean I ain't much of a threat to anyone—dosed up with all kinds of non-combat ethical routines as I am. I was just minding my own business mending fences up near Polar Flats to keep the goats from climbing off yer Highness' property when some son of a bitch plugged me a good one. Didn't even see the bastard sneak'n up on me."

"Kent will help there. Don't you worry anymore.
Likely one of the James kids. Go back to
Mending the fences that secure our goats," the King says.

Cowboy Bob nods and touches his hat, "Will do, me Lord."
The android then walks out the door and takes off sprinting at his max acceleration of 9.8 m/s, reaches a peak speed of 65 km/h, and runs off on the old dirt road that fronts the King's ranch house to mend the fences of his sovereign liege lord.

SCENE 2: NERIL AND REGAN
IN A BOAT AT NIGHT

Rocking in a small boat drenched in moonlight we see two brothers. Each has a fishing pole. Round red and white bobbers float a short distance away, the coil of a nylon fishing line spiraling in and out of the water from the pole to the strike indicator, sending off a concentric circle of benign ripples. The water is calm and glassy otherwise, except for similar disturbances launched across the water whenever the occupants move. It is well past midnight. They have come here to talk, freely. Without the net. Without any possible interference or bugging device. They've come here like they used to when they were small boys, hiding from their father and his harsh demands and dark moods. The air is fairly cool over the lake, but the water is warm. The truck that brought the load of fish from the fishery high in the Unitas unloaded them this afternoon. Those that aren't caught tonight will likely die in the next few days in the warm water. Crows will eat them. They will not go to waste.

"Is your essay done?" The speaker is Neril. One of the King's sons.

"Yeah. You?" Regan answers.

"Yup."

They are quiet awhile.

"Can you believe he's going to do it? Retire I mean. It's so unexpected."

Regan nods, "Weird even. I can't picture the old man doing it. But it seems real."

Neril's got a bite. He stands and reels frantically, rocking the boat and like to upset it. Regan grabs a long-handled net and lowers it under the fish that Neril has brought close to the boat and with a deft movement captures the large twenty-five-pound tilapia.

"Would you look at the size of that!" Neril says with some pride.

Regan says nothing but is smiling broadly.

"I'll have the Handy cook it up for tomorrow, do you and Cornflower want to bring the kids over for a fish dinner?"

"Maybe so. I'll ask her."

"Do that. Let me know."

Neril removes the hook with a tool from the bottom of an already open tackle box, then deftly rebaits his hook and casts it out a goodly distance from the boat.

They are silent awhile. Regan finally says, "They probably fed the damn things before they unloaded them."

"Probably."

"Do you remember when the King used to take us out when we were boys out to the Westwater Reservoir in that big old houseboat?" Regan says, looking out over the water, "Weren't those the days. He would sit with his guitar, and he and mom would sing songs from when they were kids."

"Remember how easily he would laugh and maybe on a lark grab us and throw us over the side and soon we were playing 'big fight on dad' and we'd try to wrestle him into the water?"

"And we never did 'till mom joined the fray, and the three of us would drag him over the side," Neril laughs.

"And Delia would cry afraid we would hurt him."

"She'd cry! That's right," Neril says shaking his head, a big smile on his face.

"I wish I'd done more of that sort of thing with my kids. It's been so busy."

"Yeah me too. The King knew how to live and make us all feel like we were living. I'll give him that."

"Until mom left."

Neril doesn't say anything but fiddles with the reel in the moonlight.

"He never got over that I think."

"Never did."

"Hester was good for him," it almost transmogrifies into a question.

"Maybe. He never did get his soft side back."

"No."

They fish for a while longer. The moon is making a slow arch across the sky. The mountains, bathed in the moonlight, show gray peaks above where the scrub stops growing. The fish aren't biting. Maybe they are dead already.

"If he goes through with it, what are you going to do with your share?" Regan turns his head and looks at Neril from the side.

"Raise goats I guess."

Silence, only a slight gurgling as the water slips under the boat.

"Me too. But do you ever get tired of it?"

Silence. Then, "You know if he heard you say that, he'd have you executed. But yeah."

"Cornflower hates 'em. The goats."

"Edda too."

"The old man never could see what this damn place was doing to everyone. Never could see how much his dream wasn't ours. You know?"

"Been thinking about that since he said he was retiring."

More silence.

"Him retiring," Regan pauses, "That's the biggest sign he ain't right."

"Hell, there are signs everywhere. His ordering that damn thing from Brazil."

"Yeah, and the way he's gone speaking in that fake poetical gibberish."

"Yeah, mad as a whale with polar encephalitis, "singing while they's beach'n" as they say and now he's doing it speaking with that crap Shakespeare shit. And that damn idiot he hangs with joined him in that la di da theater talk. What a bastard!"

They both laugh.

"Maybe it's time we followed our own life? You know?" Neril says slowly.

"Maybe. He don't care a damn about us. Not since mom left."

"Why do we owe him shit?"

The fishing is abandoned. They sit in the boat for a long time. Talking. Talking and talking and talking about that last question. Why do they owe him shit?

SCENE 3: THE LAND

Here. Here is the home of the King. High on the promontory of a stately hill that looks down on Taylor Flats Road from the foot-hills of Mann's Peak. To the Northwest, one can see the dry slopes of nearby Mt. Waas. I have traveled there in noncorporeal form often and entered in and observed the day-to-day activity of this future King (as unbound by time as I am). He is often moody and unpleasant, most find him hard to read. It is true he can change like fickle oceanic weather—one moment calm and mild, and the next an untamable tempest. While I was still a tempter, I would have played upon his inconsistency to diabolical effect—alienat-ing those who want to love him by filling his interpersonal spaces with resentment and mistrust. I suppose he's done a good enough job with this himself so maybe I would have been superfluous. But, those days are over and now I just observe. And it is for your sake that I do not intrude—so that I might be your true and unbiased omniscient narrator. A great party is about to begin. A grand affair attended by all the noble and great ones.

But before we go in. Look to the East and what do you see? A pair of visitors approaching on the backs of two reliable mules. Listen and you will hear a telling conversation lofting in on the slight wind, one moment loud, another quieter, depending on whether the wind facilitates or hinders the sound as it plays among the Gambel oak and undaunted grasses. Shall we get closer so we can hear?

—Asmodeus

SCENE 4: HESTER AND ELLIE

"What do you see in him? I'm sorry mom, I just have trouble with him. I like him, ok, but . . . " The speaker is Ellie, a young woman of about 27, the woman on the other mule is her mother Hester.

Ellie reaches down and pats the old mule as if to reassure it that the complaint in her voice was about distant concerns and not directed at the poor beast.

Hester looks at her daughter and shrugs, "He has always treated us well enough, and me especially. I suppose one does not choose love."

"Then why don't you marry him?" Ellie says with accusation in her voice.

"Young lady I do not answer to you, or anyone, about that. I have my reasons."

They plod forward in silence. The King's great house is visible as they round a low hill. It is a massive, three-story log cabin mansion modeled after the imagined hall of a Viking lord or perhaps an elfin prince's keep fashioned out of the pages of a fantasy novel. Whatever its inspiration, its aspect creates a majestic presence standing alone among the scrub, the august La Sal mountains mothering protectively over it, watching approvingly. The solar panels covering the roof give it a jeweled aspect as if it has been constructed from panels of obsidian or onyx.

Around the house, like triangular shrines built to make offerings to the greater, more honored, structure, are pitched the white tents of the Estonian refugees that he tempted here twenty years ago with promises of wages and freedom, neither of which have come in abundance. They have come to celebrate the King's birthday and have wandered from all over the La Sals for this occasion. Still, these refugees, whose land is now under thousands of feet of glaciers brought by the collapse of the Gulf Stream when the Arctic melted. They show a strange loyalty to their king. However, to Hester and Ellie, they are invisible, even though the hum of the solar air conditioning in each tent gives the distinct impression they are entering the buzzing confines of a giant apiary.

Around the house, much closer than the tents, are also heliopods, and many vehicles of various types—all denoting luxury, wealth, and power.

Hester and Ellie ride on, through the dry autumn grasses and desiccated forbs that lay resting under the scrub oak found sparsely on either side of their dirt track.

"I hate those goats," Hester says.

Scattered under the trees are the King's treasure. His beloved skin goats. His gold. His dragon's hoard. It was this wealth that made him King of the five peaks lined up behind his home. The goats shimmer in the undulant heat of the late morning, glistening dark gray in the sun, their sweating skin shining with the silky moisture leaking from their pores.

"Don't let Leere hear you say that."

Hester laughs and says, "You are right about that."

One of the goats stands and shakes itself, then walks over to a Wetgrabber Solarstill containment bucket and takes a long drink, then wanders back over to the scrub oak, and plops down again in the small tree's filigreed shade.

Hester looks from the goat to Ellie, "You're studying science, do you know whose skin they are wearing? I still find it creepy that they have human skin. It disgusts me."

Ellie nods, "I've heard that from other of you oldsters. I've never minded. But yeah, I know whose skin it was made from. It's a famous mod and is described in every biology textbook used in the uws. It was May Sope's skin, the Melanesian gene artist from the University of Chicago. It was her own sequence. Being from New Guinea, her natural skin has evolved to be perfect for the goats that have to stay in the heat all day. It has a very high concentration of melanin, plus a much higher than normal concentration of sweat glands so the goats can take advantage of the human cooling system. The odd grey color comes from some mouse genes they added to stabilize the goat/human mix."

Hester looks uncomfortable then says in a low voice, "It also feeds Leere's hatred of the Oceanic people."

"From the war?"

"Yeah. He likes the idea of the goats wearing their skins."

"Mom! That's horrible."

"Yes. I've tried to help him forgive. But terrible things happened in the war . . ." she is silent for a while then adds, "He won't forget."

"I didn't know he was filled with such vile racism. I thought the skin was all about practical survival for the goats up here."

"It's that too. But underneath it all is some terrible hurt and fear he won't shake."

Ellie looks sidelong at her mother and after a short hesitation asks, "Did they do terrible things to him in the war?"

Hester is slow to answer but finally says, almost inaudibly, "No. I think he did terrible things to them. That's the trouble. It haunts him, and there is no way to heal and he resents them for it. He's transferred his guilt into an ugly hatred for the people he's caused to suffer. He wants them to deserve what he did to them. I think deep down he wants redemption, he wants to forget, but . . . ," she trails off.

"Ugh, mom, how do you deal with it?"

"Leere has his ways. And there is more to him than his darkness. I try to bring that goodness into the light. . . Still, I find the goats disgusting in every way. That skin is so creepy. I'll never get used to it. I can't even touch it."

"Just like I'll never get used to you and the King being together."

Hester looks at her daughter with some compassion.

"When we first met I had your reaction to him. I found him arrogant and overbearing," Hester smiles remembering. "I was a believer in the church then. Very active."

"I remember that. I liked it better then." Ellie pauses as the hoof beats continue on the gravely track, then continues, "When I was little, I remember when you prayed for us. It felt like the universe was safer then. You had the power to bend God's ear to attend us."

"I know. And I'm still a believer, kiddo. It's just . . . complicated."

"Well, you're the mistress of a man that will never take you to the temple. That's got to complicate things a bit." Ellie said this without accusation and to which her mother assents with a grunt. Then continues her reminiscence.

"I was the Western States Union ambassador to the Nation of Hawaii. He had come over with his family for vacation and I hosted a big party for some of the movers and doers from the Union. The King arrived and as a good hostess, listened politely to his talk of goats and the La Sals. And what happened in the conversation, I don't know. I was smitten, he was smitten, and the next thing I knew I'd left your father and moved to Moab to be with him. I've never regretted it though. You know that."

Ellie nods, "Nor does Dad I think. You two were never meant to be together."

Hester laughs, "No. That was a disaster. But enough. What about you and Delia, is there a sealing in the temple on the horizon?"

"Mom! We are not that far along. Please don't say anything like that Ok? Please?"

Her mother rides closer to Ellie and in a conspiratorial whisper says, "Mums the word."

"Mom! Stop."

Hester laughs. "Ok."

"But if we did. It would break my heart if you weren't there."

"Your dad will be there, he keeps his recommend shiny."

"I'd like you there too if it ever happened."

Her mother says nothing and again the sound of the wind through the grasses sings a soothing hush over the rugged land. Goats are scattered here and there as part of the large herds that the King owns.

Her mother slows her mount, stops, and motions for Ellie to do the same. The house is much nearer. They will reach it soon.

"So any sense of how this will play out tonight? He's told me nothing. Nothing. Usually I can squeeze this kind of shit out of him. I thought that the King favored Neril and your sister Edda, and he would give them the good grazing near the Buckeye Reservoir, but I'm not sure anymore. Regan and Cornflower have seemed to be more in the King's affections of late. Whatever. Dividing the land is likely to cause some hard feelings don't you think? How is Delia taking it?"

"I don't know. She seems strangely subdued for someone about to inherit a fortune."

"Ah. Are you marrying her for her money?"

"Yes. Mom. That's it. I'm marrying her for her money. Would you leave it? You're bechdelling up this whole conversation. We. Are. Not. Talking. About. Marriage . . . Yet anyway. ok?"

Hester smiles, "Ok. Got it. Of course, I never planned on leaving Hawaii either . . . "

"Mom!"

ACT III

LEERE'S RANCH HOUSE
IN THE LA SALS

SCENE I: THE STAGE IS SET!

*T*he stage is set! *The lighting, managed by the late afternoon sun hidden behind the mountains, gives our players a spectral backlit glow that no stage manager could ever hope to arrange. The dusty haze infesting the sky in this part of the world weakens the sun, but gives the sunset a gorgeous bloody, orange tint, enhancing significance and the promise of a glorious future, or apocalyptic endings, depending on your inclination.*

The King's Hall is festooned with kudzu from the Northern Confederation interwoven with sparkling purple and gold solstice-lights. Hung throughout the chamber are commissioned tapestries tastefully depicting skin-goats standing majestically on various promontories found throughout the La Sals. These are elaborately bordered with scenes from the King's life. Stitched in bright colors against a dark blue and earthy umber background, suggesting in understated textures a sense of nobility and an atmosphere of regal formality. A minstrel rock band is quietly and tastefully playing old favorites Leere has personally picked out and in some cases arranged. Estonian servants are making the rounds among the guests, offering delicacies from all over the world: dodo eggs from Mauritius, Turkish Delight from Disney Narnia, pâté de foie gras from France (not bio-printed, but made from the livers of real geese), dimes of Montana bison served on water crackers spread with brie, grapes from Senegal, fine Chinese wines, and New Zealand beers.

Almost everyone is dressed in formal wear. So grand is the pomp and pageantry of this fete that the attire of those assembled make even Academy Awards seem a shabby, and maudlin affair—women in elegant evening wear, men in tuxedos and cowboy boots. Prominent people from all over the Union are standing around eating and talking and enjoying themselves. Three senators (Wyoming, Utah, and Oregon) and the Mayors of Salt Lake and Reno are here (both, in an embarrassing coincidence, are adorned in stunning Carl Overton designed dresses). Several foreign dignitaries have also come to celebrate with the King, including the Colorado Ambassador and a dignitary from Argentina's Ministry of Commerce. At the King's request, everyone has tuned their neural implants to an app especially commissioned by Leere. It has the effect on the visual cortex of representing all the servants dressed in the livery of an 18th Century house staff. It also creates a hallucination of naked cherubs flying about the room launching volleys of golden arrows at the guests. As incongruent as it sounds, given the other effects, the app also occasionally creates the illusion of bandits who suddenly pour into the room and shoot up the place until a sheriff and his posse arrive to take them down. If you are shot by one of the hooligans, the servants will ignore you for five minutes. Although, the guests are, for the most part politely using the app as requested, just in case the King has some relevant content to share, they are mostly ignoring the annoying shenanigans being generated in their visual field.

However, it is not these we must focus on. No. We must turn our attention to Leere's family gathered in this hall. They alone are the principal actors of this prearranged theatrical production. The king sits in his great recliner, a beer in the cup holder, and, what is this? Indeed, you are not mistaken, it is a smile on his face. Unlike his guests, he is dressed in new deep blue boot-cut Levis, a loose T-shirt adorned with a picture of a goat head nobly tilted to the sky bleating freedom into the air; the letters "La Sal Goat Company" forming a half circle above the bearded beast. His refusal to don formal wear is well known and his wealth allows him and his own to entertain such eccentricities. On his lap is a felt cowboy hat, comfortable sandals adorn his feet (the app also puts him in cowboy boots as he finds them too uncomfortable to actually wear). He is in a rare mood, and I with my demonic powers hear his inner monolog loud, he is almost shouting the lines from A Midsummer's Night Dream, "Come, sit down, every mother's son, and rehearse your parts." He thinks he is about to produce a play. Ha! He is about to be buried by one.

Beside him on a matching leather chair is his paramour Hester Glock who you've met riding in with her daughter Ellie, (Her great-grandmother changed their name from Bloch to Glock to help her descendants remember which pistol was her favorite). She is dressed casually, wearing a sequin decorated turquoise cotton skirt, a T-shirt that matches that of the king, and short cream white cowboy boots. Unlike Leere, she is not relaxed. This is clear from the way she sits, her feet stiffly planted on the floor, her hands gripping the arms of the chair just a little too tightly; a slight twitch under her eye; and other signs of discomfort too minor to bother detailing, but as your *omniscient narrator, I can do better. I can tell you causes underlying her nervousness. She has much at stake. Her daughter, Edda is married to the King's son and, therefore, the young lady's fortunes are tied to her husband, Regan. Her other daughter is clearly in love with the King's daughter Delia. How will this play out? What if Regan is given Buckeye, the last standing water in the La Sals? She has offered her opinion on the dividing to the King but he barked that she is not allowed to meddle in these affairs.*

There, next to the King, is "The Fool." The heretic who refused to follow the Missouri LDS President Hoag in allowing transgenic humans to be baptized regardless what part animal they contained or what percentage their genetics were lifted from non-humans.

After the fool's fall from grace from the LDS Church proper, and his instinctive hatred of the more liberal EDA Church, he wandered through the wastelands of the earth. He stumbled through the wilderness, alone, in poverty and in search of, as he said, true doctrine. He went to India for a while to study the Gita. He followed the Spockist Stoics for a time in Bankok, framing his life by logic and appetite control. At last, broken he came to the King's table where he has remained to amuse and goad the old goatherd. He is a tall, bent and ancient sage, with a glorious beard that spills to his waistline like a wizard's. He dresses only in a thigh-length dressing gown of royal purple edged with a yellow fur, and sporting striped socks that ride to his knees. What the old master sees in him all his children wonder for the fool seems well named. And even Leere's girlfriend cannot abide the dolt. Yet in his grace the King grants him sanctuary, for he appreciates the Fool's stance on human purity and in his lands no half-humans will ever dwell. Leere hates them as much as does the fool. A true friend to the King, he reminds him to be humble and attend to his spiritual side. It was for such boldness the heretic lost both place and position in both the recreated Church Office Building in Independence Missouri for apostasy, and the EDA temple in Salt Lake City by inclination.

There sitting opposite the King's comfortable recliners are his sons. Regan and Neril. Both are hoping they will get control of Buckeye Reservoir, an important resource of necessary and scarce water. However, and here is the rub, unbeknownst to the King, but which I scry perfectly, they have both connived to sell their portions as soon as the lawyers put the final touches on their inheritance and it is in their hands. To hell with the old king they both have agreed. Whatever fealty they owe him was paid by having to live under his shadow all this time. He is as despised under their smiles, as one of the great pale turds the goats drop all over this land—The land the King loves. The land the King worships therefore will be sold to the highest bidder by his loving sons. Once sold, Regan plans to buy a villa on the Buford Sea; Neril plans to open an import business in southern Chile. As I look into their sadly bitter hearts, I sense that they are full of greed and vitriol—as only a former daemon can properly appreciate. If I am honest, the stench they radiate from their twisted souls almost tempts me back to my relinquished occupation. What evil could be wrought with their wealth and power! Was it not that which caused the great warming in the first place? Oh, yes, it tempts a daemon greatly to see such heartless greed graced with such wealth and power! But no. I shake myself. I am done. I sigh, dismissing the temptations of my youth. And now I realize with some clarity, that even these sons harbor some complexity worth attending. Were they made this way by the King? What part of their anger can be laid at their feet and what portion his? Note this well from a former daemon. Whenever evil appears utter, search your own heart to see what it excludes.

Neril's wife Edda, the daughter of Hester, is the mirror of her husband. She has decorated their home with art from the Antarctic seas near where they will live once they are rid of these barren desert mountains. However, she also loves the flora and fauna and fashion of the cold North and hopes to replicate it in Chile where they plan to dwell. Their home smells of the sea (generated by a diffuser). Seashells, driftwood, lemming bone lattice-statues of many of the extinct animals of the North: Polar bears, musk ox, and walruses. But her favorite work of art is her scale model Viking ship. She loves the Vikings and fashions herself a Valkyrie of a sort. In spirit, she is not far off the mark. At least in her desire to conquer, even if it takes raids and bloodshed.

Regan's wife, Cornflower James, is a local girl. Her father owns the land from below Taylor flats down into Paradox Valley. Although neither would admit it, especially to themselves, theirs was a political marriage. The King and Cornflower's father, Big D. James, had worked hard to bring them together because they believed that it would repair the conflicts that had plagued the two towering personalities and their constant disputes over water, property lines, road access, and a thousand other contentions both big and small. Sadly the marriage has done nothing to repair the tensions, and the King's feud with the Jameses is as fierce and unholy as ever. None of the other Jameses are present at these festivities. No one really knows where her loyalties stand. Not even her husband. Not even me, an omniscient narrator. Omniscience has its hidden spaces (Isn't that where they say evil lies—the holes which God has left and cannot penetrate).

In the corner sits a mousy woman in a business suit. She is nondescript, expressionless, and draws no attention to herself. She sits in a chair in the corner waving off the occasional Estonian server that dares approach. She is the King's lawyer—Maggie Brim. She is superb at what she does, and he pays her well for it.

The guests and family have gathered. Let the curtain rise!

—Asmodeus

SCENE 2: THE KING PROCLAIMS
THE LAND IS TO BE DIVIDED

A gong calls everyone into the main hall. From his throne, a large chair on a dais arranged in the front of the room, the King gazes with paternal affection at his family gathered to honor him and receive his blessing. They have taken front row seats on stiff straight-backed chairs fashioned from velvet and silver—stately, though a bit uncomfortable. The guests have also gathered in the hall and are seated behind his children and their families on plastic pews set up for the occasion.

All present are smiling amicably, he notes, save only Delia, who seems, unusually, morose and distracted. He will not let her mood spoil his own. Tonight he will formally divide his land among his children. His lawyer sits to the side, fierce, and authoritative. She is set to add her official seal on the transaction about to occur. Once things are done, they are done for good. Leere takes one more long drink of beer and stands up and imperially motions with his hand. There is immediate silence. All his children and their present spouses attend to his words as if he were one of the ancient prophets. He speaks.

> "Know my children that on this day you will
> Receive that grand inheritance, made bright
> For your good glory. I glad retire."

There was a small gasp from the audience at this unexpected news. Only his children knew what was coming.

"Let not this difficulty raise your ire."

There were mock murmurs and small protests at his words from among his children and family as if to say, "You are far too young to do this! Stay your hand dear father we are not ready for your abdication!" He waves off these hollow objections by just holding up his hand.

> "Proclaim I now, Hester and I will bow
> Out. We beg a small goat herd to retain,
> A hundred stout Slavic goatherds ably,
> Kept about our cabin near Hidden Lake
> That I might the passion of youth enjoy
> And keep my hands full at goat husbandry.
> Reserve I keen the right to travel free
> Over my long-held domains without bound
> To stride among my favored sites nestled
> In these glorious hills. But this you know.
>
> On then, to that fair business at hand—
> Time to divide these my holdings amongst
> My children brave, asked I only that each should
> From scratch an essay write honoring this
> Great land—to speak boldly of their bright love
> For home, and this land's true nurture. To each
> According to his or hers excellence
> And grace I will apportion these fair tracts.
> Never from them again to make demands."

Even though all his children know this was coming, there is a nervous pause at the realization that their inheritance might be determined by their skills in written expression. Of course, his sons each secretly believe that surely this has all been determined beforehand, that these essays are a mere formality, but even so there is enough room for doubt that a giddy anxiety permeates the air. Regan and Neril, at least, can feel some comfort in that they did their very best to prepare. By prepare I mean they had both paid professional writers to create their works. It was tricky because they needed to strike a balance between not looking too good—their father knows his children's capabilities—and being moving and expressive enough to capture the old man's heart. His love for the land is fathomless. Playing on that will be the order of the day.

The old man says with imposing portent,

"Neril, my oldest, lead the way. Read on!"

He then returns to his large leather chair, stretches out his crossed legs, and places his index fingers together forming the steeple of the nursery rhyme and puts them under his chin, and nods at his son. Neril steps up, faces the crowd, appropriately nervous, and then smiles.

SCENE 3: NERIL'S ESSAY

Father, my thesis is this: I love this land more than words can frame the weighty matter. Since I was a lad, my eyes have happily gazed on these bold granite mountains. I have been enraptured by the vaulted blue sky that blesses the dome of the carbuncle heavens with unfettered joy. For it is in this good soil that you planted my soul at an early age. You watered it with the clear, abundant moisture pulled from the air, and stored it in the artificial aquifer that you have fashioned out of living rock.

This place was waste and doom until you searched the wide earth to find a beast that could in these desert blasted lands dwell. You had your setbacks. The Zebu cattle you brought from the Sahel of Senegal withered and died on this dusty plain, their bones still litter the sides of these great laccoliths, and by that, we know that you would do anything to make this land bear fruit.

But you did not give up as you were warned again and again to do. I was five when you brought the Iberian Ibex from the spare and wild Holy Land in hopes that that blessed goat of the Negev might in the brittle grasses of this dying land find sustenance. But it was not to be, for its hollow carcasses soon littered this land beside the cattle, their skin stretched tight across their ant-savaged bones.

A lesser man would have given up in sorrow, my Father, and in despair proclaim, "There is no livestock fit for this land." But you are not that man Father, and in you there arose a warrior-like spirit, as if the sea-kings of old who faced whatever elements they were handed with courage and daring had been remade among the shadows of these hills. Was it not you, Father, who asked the scientists what could be done? Did you not plant within them this question, How might we manufacture a beast who could live in such haunts as this? Like a Viking king of old who inspires his smiths to make a new kind of sword and lighter armor, you lifted the hearts of the geneticists, and begged them, rise to the challenge and find a way to make a goat that could survive this koch-blighted land. And they found one! The rise of skin-goats became your passion and from their meat and milk, you made a kingdom to rival the court of Charlemagne of old.

And have you not taught me to love this land? To hold the values you have taught me? To believe that no land was beyond redemption and forgiveness? Have you not found a profit where none dared look? And so this land I have learned to love beyond eyesight. No less than life, with grace, health beauty, honor. What will I do with this land when it is mine? Why, of course, I will do as you have done. For by my lights this land is naught but a reflection of you! Your lines and crevasses are mirrored in the land's. So I will cherish the work that you have chosen as I cherish you. I will act as you have acted. I can do nothing but what I have seen my Father do, as Jesus said, and so this too is my motto.

In short, I see the mountains filled with goats. I envision their nourishing meat eaten throughout the Union of Western States, From Northern and Southern California to lands of Latin Confederacy and as far away as China and the Island nations. So this is my pledge to you, dear Father. When I have my portion, I will do as you have done—with a wish only to expand your vision. To find genes to splice into these hardy varieties and bless them with new and more clever traits to make their survival more secure and their future sure.

Your work is all I wish. I love this land in ways that my poor breath takes flight as I try to write this essay to tell you that this land is loved. Valued with a heart both full and richly blessed. And by a Father who showed me how it was to be done.

SCENE 4: THE KING IS PLEASED

When Neril finishes, amid the applause of the captive crowd, the King leaps to his feet and rushes to embrace his son. Leere holds him for several minutes. One would have to know the King very well not to look to see if he was weeping.

"Well said, my goodly son, well said indeed," the old king shouts holding his boy at arms length and looking at his face. The King returns to his chair as does Neril. As the King's son sits down, few observe that Edda grabs his thigh just above his knee and gives a hard squeeze. "Nice!" she whispers smiling.

The Heretic Fool shakes his head and says grumpily,

"Old man careful be. For such flattery reigns
In verbiage thick. And as the Psalmist cries, Pride
Before the Fall goeth! Stand thou unmoved."

"As you would know about such falls," the King says smiling, "as you know!"

Delia is staring straight ahead, detached from the scene she has just witnessed. A strange, almost rebellious look graces her face.

The King then takes a long drink of his dark brew. Seeing his glass is now empty, one of the Estonian household servants quickly moves to replace it. The fool grabs it for his own, saying, "The needs of the one, outweigh the needs of the many." before the King can reach out his hand, but another was quickly provided to replace it.

The old man then points to Regan smiling.

"You're up!"

SCENE 5: REGAN'S ESSAY

Good Father. You know I do not have the skill of words my good brother has. And yet I find he comes too short in his praise of this land. It is my thesis that this land has never been better. Once, they say it ran with water of its own accord. That scrawny skeletal aspens once hugged the sides of these godly hills. That pines made the vast valleys somehow better and richer. Nonsense say I. Nonsense I shout with boldness. Who benefited from these "greener" hills? Whose lives were made richer? A few hunters? A few cattleman perhaps? But they just scratched the surface of the potential of these hills. They could not even pay their taxes without selling the land off piece by piece (or how else could the wisdom of my Father-King have bought it from under their unproductive noses).

The land is better now for it is feeding the world! It is providing gainful employment for refugees who otherwise would starve. Bully on you Father! For now, every year, hundreds of thousands of goats are feeding the hungry world. I've been there when the great airships of the abattoir land and weigh anchor. I have seen their quick work in loading their frozen holds with meat that you have provided. That you make possible with your skill in managing these wondrous lands.

And while it might make silly women squirm, I've also seen that the skins are wasted. Why this is illegal in so many states I do not understand. They are not human skins! They are protein bundles constructed from nucleotides, that, yes we do share sequences with, but surely that does not make them human sequences, or the skins human skins. I will not just carry on your work Father, but I will fight to correct the laws that keep you from making your maximum profit. All here know that they are not "discarded" by the abattoirs. They are sold in the Far East to great advantage of which we get but a pittance. I love this land enough to ensure that what comes of it, comes back to us.

And so as you have shown, Father, my love of the land reflects a love of what the land can do. Of what can be brought to bear from its use. So as my brother fell short in his praise of the land, he falls short of grasping its potential and worth!

If I am given this land, I will do as you have done, Father. You were given five talents, Father and returned ten again as a faithful servant should. Give me those ten talents and I will return the original ten and twenty more yet again. Such any can do who truly love the land as you have. I will not just carry on your given legacy, I will take your spirit and attitudes and see what glory those attributes continued will bring forth from these holy hills. I have a father who will spare no expense to protect his legacy! I will do likewise. Like you, I will hold these lands with whatever weapons it takes. I am proud to be the son of a warrior.

SCENE 6: DELIA'S REFUSAL
AND VIDEO OF BETTER TIMES

The King stands deliberately. He claps slowly, wagging his head in admiration, almost imitating a behavior of the goats he loves. This action is usually reserved for those times when he is deeply moved, as when a new kind of goat is introduced to strengthen the herd. He then holds his arms open wide laughing. He loves his boys. Most excellent boys they are. He is proud.

"Well said! Well said indeed. Much yet to be,
Squeezed there is from this fine and holy land."

Cornflower is grinning from ear to ear as her husband moves to his father and embraces him tightly.

"Sons like this, portend goodly and rich lands
Managed well and in most excellent hands.
There is future in these hills; goats galore!"

Only Neril and Edda seem displeased. Both of them glaring at Regan, that is until their father looks at them. Then suddenly their lips loosen into a pleasant smile and they join the applause.

Hester does not seem to share her daughter Eda's displeasure, at least outwardly, and is looking at the King with a large smile on her face, as if she is enjoying the entertainment.

"Come. We have one more work to consider.
Delia. It is your turn."

"I have no essay, sir."

"What do you mean? I sent you the email
One month past. Answer me, have you done
Nothing? Have you put no effort into
It at all. Show me your first drafts at least."

"I have nothing."

"Nothing?"

"Nothing."

The King looks genuinely confused. He turns to his partner Hester and she seems as surprised as he is, she looks at Ellie, who is staring at Delia with the same shocked expression so common to the murmurers whose whispers are whisking around the room.

> "Delia, dear, the rules were made. You must strive,
> Convince me that you love the land as much
> As I, at least if you a share desire.
> Nothing comes of nothing. Come now. Give your
> Part extemporaneously. You are
> An able university woman.
> Show your father what cunning sophistry
> You can conjure on the fly to show me
> That your love of the land is like my own."

The King fidgets nervously smiling in turn at each of the other participants as if waiting for one of them to reveal the joke that Delia is playing.

Delia stands with her head bowed. But says nothing.

"Then you most sadly do not love this land."

"Not this land, Father. No, I love what it was. What it might become again, but as it stands now? No, I do not love it. My heart for this lands runs in a different direction than yours."

She looks up and pulls out a remote on which she clicks a button. A giant screen descends facing the audience and springs to life.

"This is the land I love."

On the screen is a timeworn video. It shows a young man standing in front of the lush foliage of a leafy tree. He is wearing cargo shorts and a T-shirt with a tropical frog peering out.

"It's May 24, 2028. The aspen tree behind me is made of 432 individuals of varying ages, some nearly seventy-five years old. The last few winters have been warm enough to keep the fungal disease active and the borer problem to become more pronounced. Since last year, 12% of the trees have died from the disease. Additionally, because the cattle ranchers refuse to give up their allotment, the drought has put pressure on the elk herds here in the La Sals and they have been stripping the bark off of many of the trees. That accounts for another 7% tree loss."

The video jumps ahead, and begins another segment. Then another . . .

"It's May 22, 2029 . . .

"It's May 26, 2030 . . .

"It's May 23, 2041,

"It's May 24, 2052,

"It's May 30, 2063. They are all dead. The aspen grove that has been the focus of my dissertation and early career at U. Mass is gone." The researcher in the video pauses to collect himself, with a catch in his voice he continues.

"The Hadley cell that once stood over the Sonoran Desert has expanded faster than the models predicted and has turned the chaparral that has defined the climate of these magnificent laccoliths for ten thousand years into a desert. There will be little moisture here, save the summer monsoons, which will be brief violent and destructive. The carbon is at 550 and there is little hope that this ecosystem can be saved, especially with the release of the methane reserves in the tundra. The aspens are gone. All of them. I cannot find a single grove and I feel like my heart is breaking. The elk, deer, have followed under the pressure of the cattlemen who have tried to keep their grazing rights alive in this blotted land, but now too they are dropping off the land. I've not seen a deer prancing through the meadows here since 2021. My colleague, mammalogist Manda

Rencher believes they are all gone. Invasive grasses dominate now and the once lush ponderosa forests have been replaced with Gambel's oak, sage, and cheatgrass." The man suddenly sat on the ground and wept. The video played a few more seconds then ended.

The room is silent. The King starts to shake. He is livid. The outrage flares from the redness of his face, from the clenching of his fists, and his jaw muscles look so strained that Hester worries it might break his teeth.

Delia looks at the King with concern.

"Father this is the land I love. This is what I believe we could do again. Carbon has shrunk to 500 under the strong mandates of the world powers and with it maybe the Hadley circulation will go back, some models say it will be so. Do they not? There is hope that if we could let the land recover, that these ecosystems could be redeemed! They can be restored. I do not want land to make goat meat. I want to return it to what it was. Make again the forests of pine and fir, high meadows, and lakes that stay year round. I want aspens Father. The white bark, the shimmering leaves of spring and the gold of late autumn. I want to make the forests magical again! I want to see Dark Canyon dark again with verdant undergrowth, and streams with trout, chad, and sculpins; living rivulets whose stone bottoms are green with moss and mayfly larvae. I want bears to roam these mountains feasting on a variety of wild berries which flood the valleys in the Fall. I want wildflowers exploding year round in reds, violets, blues, yellows, and whites. I want elk to whistle loud and free during the rut and the hills to be alive with their lust and love of life. Father this is what I love. Not an ecosystem depauperate and empty of its potential. But one rich with life and abundant with the green things of the world. Can you not see it? Goats do not matter. They will keep this land ugly and waste. Let us seek the land's redemption. Its resurrection. Is it so impossible to imagine?"

The King rises, unsteadily, the first sign that age is having its way with him. He usually hides it and its presence brokers his wrath, he has never shown weakness in public. The room is both shocked and delightfully entertained at the turn of events.

"Delia, mean you this horror that you speak?"

"Yes. With all my heart I speak what I truly feel."

The old man falls back into his seat. Hester reached to comfort him but he waves her away.

"Be it so then, the embrace of that vile
Feeling will be thine inheritance full.
I thought a blessed daughter I had raised,
But I see only a spoiled girl child.
A cruel and unholy fiend. Or idiot!
By the stars and moon, with thee I am done.
I loved you better than either of my sons
And with this falseness I am well repaid?"

As he said this, he picks up a ceramic pot and made as if to throw it, when the KENT battle dredge who had been standing in the corner monitoring, speaks, "Majesty, she is on the list of protected humans, shall I override that protection to allow your threat to her person?"

The King falls back into his seat and covers his eyes with his hands saying

"Do not intervene, but remove the witch from
The list of those care I most about and offer
Full protection. Make her as one of the
Estonians. This onetime fair daughter
Will no longer have place in my aged heart."

Everyone is frozen.

Delia weeping says, "Father this is not what I want. I cannot be like my brothers, I care for this land more than life, but I cannot say in honesty that you care as I do or I care as they do. Please."

"Go."

"But Father, where?"

"I don't care." Then he turned to the shocked assembled guests,

"Will any have her?
Will any of you offer her place?
She will not have one here. It is thus lost."

Her brothers look uncomfortable but say nothing. They hide how pleased they are at this turn of events. Hester is making grouper like motions with her mouth, but nothing is coming out.

Ellie is in a rage. She begins accusing the King loudly, "Here's a strange thing. A few minutes ago she was the best of your children, your dearest! And yet in an instant, she is nothing? You are no Father. You are nothing but old and broken goatherd. As senile as they claim, speaking such rhymes while sending your beloved daughter to hell."

A few mock gasps follow from the guests, now growing more and more uncomfortable, looking toward the exits for an escape from this unpleasantness.

Delia looked grateful but gently placed her hand on Ellie's arm, "Please. My father is not yet himself."

"Not yet myself? You know nothing of my
Nature. You my whole life have insulted.
My work. And most offensive you reject
My land. I tell you again, Go. Will no
One escort this Grendel from my hall?"

Ellie walks over and places her hand on her arm, "Come with me Delia. You don't have a place here for now, but I would be glad to share your life. Come to my home in Moab."

All could tell there was more meaning in this than an offer of a place to stay. Delia with tears takes Ellie's hand.

As they walked out, Ellie turns and says to the King, "You have lost greater in this action than you are giving to your sons. Far greater."

And with that they exit.

The King is breathing hard, and takes to his throne. A sudden and unmistakable aging seems to have taken place. Even so, he is ready again to rule. "Bring up the Property Map of the La Sals."

On the big screen a map of the La Sals appears. The mountains are shaded in three colors representing the division of the land as it was to be when it was to be partitioned into thirds. Buckeye had been earmarked for Delia. If one were paying close attention, one could detect a stir of indignation from Leere's sons. Now he growls at his lawyer, "Maggie,"

"Attending."

"I want Delia's land now fair split among
Neril and Regan. Cut Buckeye North and South
And give to each an equal proportion
Of the high mountain lake whose waters
All love and honor for its use and play.

"How does this look?" his lawyer asks after tapping a computer a few times. On the computer screen there are now only two colors.

Regan interrupts, "If I may make a suggestion to the proposed ..."

Neril interrupts Regan's interruption, "I think we need to let Father do this without our interference ..."

Regan offers, "Obviously, you think that because the stream that feeds Buckeye would fall on your land ..."

"Cease and stay fiends, both of you. It is what
It is. Not another word shall be spoken.
Maggie, draw up the papers just. I wish
Only to retain my house for Hester,
For as long as it stands she may dwell in
Safety and delight in her aged dotage.
To Hell with Delia. By tonight's bad end
My bight sons anon the La Sals are thine,
As well, me thinks, the greatest goatherd west
Of the Atlantic Ocean and all the
Property wherein those blessed beasts dwell.
Delia will not again by me be glimpsed!"

He beams at them for the munificent generosity he has just manifest. Although if one looks closely at his shaded eyes, and examines them with care, one might be able to detect one of his rare doubts. And a bit of slippage in his grasp of reality.

ACT IV

TEXTING

TEXTS: REGAN AND NERIL

REGAN: He's gone to bed. Are we agreed? We act as one?

NERIL: K's sentimentality pathetic & showed aged foolishness.

REGAN: True that.

NERIL: Ha! Delia's land chunk Megagone. We score!

REGAN: True that.

NERIL: Any word?

REGAN: Offer coming now . . .

.

.

.

REGAN: Get ready 2 shit yourself.

REGAN: Yours 2.3 Billion Goldbacked Reals

REGAN: Mine 2.1 Billion Goldbacked Reals

REGAN: I'd resent your's is more but what's 0.2 Billion among bros.

NERIL: I just did shit myself. With or Without goats?

REGAN: Without. We'll make a bundle selling off the whole herd first.

NERIL: The old man w/kill us

REGAN: He's senile. Don't care. He's not even all there. He won't see a doc but I'm sure he has the Alz. Can you see him flaming D like that just a few years ago? An old goat. Don't matter w/ he thinks. We own it now can't do a damned thing. What about his bitch? She's your in-law, Bro

NERIL: We got ideas

REGAN: We need her property they don't want to dig the rare earths around her and you can't level the mountain with her sitting on it

NERIL: I said we got ideas

TEXTS: EDDA LIES TO ELLIE

EDDA: It went full crazy after you left he sent the Battle Dredge after Delia.

ELLIE: WTF?

EDDA: Full on. He's raging, you heard him take off her protection from the bot? You better hide her good.

Ellie: I took her to my house in Moab. Would it come there?????

EDDA: Think Sis He knows that's where you said you'd go.

ELLIE: Didn't Mom try to stop hm?????

EDDA: She's flipped. Mad as a hornet at you for supporting Delia.

ELLIE: But she knows how I feel about her? Is the report true 2 that his Bot kill't some of the James?

EDDA: Yeah Ready's dead & Mom's old school she's said nothing to you, but she ain't down with you & Delia being a thing. She used the old handle Lesbo in front of me. You'd better hide. The King has changed her too much. She's gone dark. She said after yout left she don't want nothing more to do with you. You are dead to her. Don't matter what happens to you.

ELLIE: She said that????

EDDA: Yup

ELLIE: My heart is breaking.

EDDA: Going to be more than that if y don't get out of there.

ELLIE: Is the bot after both of us or just Delia?

EDDA: It's got your image Sis. Likely it's loaded with two targets.

EDDA: This can't be happening. Where should I go?

EDDA: What about your cabin up at Don's Lake?

ELLIE: Good ida.

EDDA: Disguise yourself. You're on target. Full on. And turn off your phone FGS.

ELLIE: I'm Scared.

EDDA: I think that's the proper response

TEXTS: EDDA LIES TO HESTER

HESTER: Have you heard from Ellie?

EDDA: Mom are you OK?

HESTER: I can't get a hold of Ellie, have you heard from her? I can't seem to reach her.

EDDA: Mom, you might want to leave her be for a bit.

HESTER: Why would you say that?

EDDA: She's got a bear up hr butt about the way the King treated Delia. She thinks you agree.

HESTER: She of all people should know me and the King disagree a lot.

EDDA: Mom she's saying terrible things about yoou.

HESTER: What do you mean? Like what.

EDDA: Mom don't make me repeat them.

HESTER: I want to know! What she saying.

EDDA: Mom, listen I wouldn't say this unless I was a little afraid. Just lay low for awhile. OK? Sometimes when people are mad they go a little crazy. You know? In pain they say things they don't mean. It's

HESTER: It's what? Are you still there?

EDDA: Yes.

HESTER: It's what?

. . .

EDDA: It's just I don't know Delia. When she says crazy things about hurting the King I don't know if she is serious. I know when Ellie says things like that about you, well she's just blowing off steam. But Delia. I don't know what she means by the threats.

HESTER: Edda, listen to me carefully. What did they say. I need to know.

EDDA: Well, they are getting some high power lawyers from Salt Lake City. They plan to have the King's will invalidated. Say he's crazy and should be locked up.

HESTER: That's terrible. And not true!

EDDA: That's not all Mom.

HESTER: Just tell me straight.

EDDA: They are planning to say you are crazy too.

HESTER: What!!!!?

EDDA: I know thy don't stand a chance, but, well, thy plan to put you two away for a long time and take the land and sell it.

HESTER: Listen. Edda. Thank you for telling me this. Don't tell your sister we talked. Please keep this under your hat. I'm going to go find Leere and get his advice. I love you. Bye.

EDDA: ILY2 Mom. I won't tell.

DAEMON'S INTERLUDE II

GREED

*T*oday *as daemons are wont to do, I wandered. In the valley next door to Castle Valley is a delightful little romp through some magnificent desert territory. Professor Creek carries cold, clear runoff nearly year round down from the La Sals. It runs below Adobe Mesa through some sublime deep canyons, relatively isolated in late autumn. I only went up as far as Mary's Falls, which splashes cold into a small pool in which I love to bathe. The water is bracing and draws off an abundance of lethargy and cleanses away the stolid heaviness that seems to afflict me from time to time. Perhaps I'm starting to love the world; just as I see it transitioning from what I know here now and what I see coming in the King's time. I feel . . . what? Resentment? Weariness? I'm not sure. I've begun to see the beauty in you. A horrible thought, but what amazing apes you are. Your art and philosophy! Your untamed curiosity that launches you into the cold vacuum of space just to see what's there. Isn't that wonderful! But then you are low and mean apes as well. So vicious; so quick to destroy what you do not understand. So tinged with hate and vitriol at those you imagine want to take* *a crumb away from your table. Apes who give little thought for futures that you can control, and so much thought for a past you cannot. What strange mixes you are of glory and hell. No wonder the great God fights over you and His Adversary relishes your company and worship.*

The falls pour over my head. I feel baptized. Cleansed from the sin of hoping too many things of you. Redeemed from expecting too much. A cold reality sets in and I remember that in the grand scheme of things neither you nor your world count for much. The universe teems with life. It comes and goes as suns and planets come exploding into existence and then pop out again sometimes with a whimper and others with a bang. Why should I let your demise ruin a lovely hike, on a particularly striking day, in a late autumn early in the 21st Century when it is decades before you slip tragically away under the weight of your own foolish desire and greed?

—Asmodeus

ACT V

ATTACK ON JAMES AT THE EDGE OF LEERE'S PROPERTY LINE IN THE LA SALS

SCENE 0: DAEMON'S OPENING

*H*ere *I must draw on all my skill as an omniscient narrator, for it is here we encounter an event so singular that it will change the evolutionary trajectory, and even the existence, of the entire La Sals. Certainly, the events will flit down upon the people we have encountered in this tale—but in a hundred years? What will it matter in ten thousand? Nothing of this place will be remembered? In 10 million, no example of your species will be around to tell the tale, sadly new warps and weaves will have structured the topology of life on earth. Time will have folded organic matter into new patterns to dance the dance.*

I get ahead of myself. We daemons can grow rather untethered in time, and it is hard, sitting here in my trailer in Castle Valley in the twenties of the new century, to remember that your concerns are with the immediacy of this present. As it should be. Indeed, as it should be.

Well, onward.

As your narrative guide, our first stop will be a mule upon which a boy rides. It will be brief. The mind of a mule has limits, and in this particular mule, they are significant. I'll follow that with my perspective on the Bucky round used on the mule. Next KENT. *Then one of the Jameses. Then the joy of a BattleDredge as it glories in its success. I get somewhat giddy thinking about the mind of that machine. It is beautiful in ways that attract and horrify me.*
—Asmodeus

SCENE I: PERSPECTIVE OF A MULE

In the mind of a mule, no human concepts frame the interplay among the neural processes that structure the underlying logical progression of its protolanguage (such as it is). However, it has mulish equivalents. For example, look there, on the side of the road, a bit of wild alfalfa. Observed, impressions from reflected light run from retina to visual cortex where images are constructed using a combination of memory and sensation to create an intentional frame that allows the good mule to attend to the plant. The motivations that arise are conditioned on its current states of hunger, its sense of the cost of stopping—as paid in the currency of harassment from the rider who is trying to keep the beast focused on the path, or in its own weighting of mulish desires and concerns. A good phenomenologist considering the effect of this mental interplay, perhaps in a kind of equine epoche, would recognize in the mule's embodied stance a not unfamiliar umbratic human counterpart in the dim traces of a conscious field. Motivations might arise to procure the fodder as it turns its attention to

characteristically plant-shaped food lying green in the shadow
of a lonely scrub oak. It stops and pulls it up with its teeth.
That favored food item starts a cascade of complex chemical
triggers that satisfy and please the beast. Because it desires
more, hormones mix with its complex neurology, the neurons
of which have begun to fire insistently, creating a calculus
inclining the mule to move forcefully toward the plant for
another bite, despite the pull of the reins resisting its forward
motion. It wants that food and is willing to pay some expense
in discomfort in order to test the rider's will in an act of defi-
ance—it is only a boy after all and the mule has enough grasp
of human attributes that it recognizes that a young human
can exert less command than an adult. It strains down and
with its teeth pulls the plant up by the roots and chews, the
action of which, in combination with olfactory neurons in its
thick tongue, sets off a small number of pleasure neurons, all
firing to bring the reward of pleasure that such a rare and significant thing was obtained. It takes another step.† It feels a

---

†. I must pause here. It is important enough information that I
ought to just include it in the text, but I do feel some responsibility as a
narrator to demand some flow without needless asides. It is that mule's
step that makes me pause, however, because it draws a thoughtful person to its hoof and away from my main thread. A mule's hoof is worth
considering for a moment. It is such a marvelously ingenious device. A
near perfectly designed gadget that acts as pad, springboard, protective
covering. Two phalanx bones connect to the distal coffin bone, which
looks like a hoof in miniature. These have evolved from the single digit
of a five-fingered toe. Think of it. A single digit. A single toe or finger
bone supports the full weight of these magnificent equines, which balance on that toe like a ballerina poised in fleshy slippers that protected it
from the shock of plodding along through life. The entire hoof is encased
in a chitin shell which protects it and provides support for whatever

confusing and disorienting sensation. It is unpleasant. A small panic begins to unravel its calm. Then all sensation stops. It is without conscious awareness. It falls dead upon the path.

SCENE 2: PERSPECTIVE OF THE BULLET

The Bucky Xm round was developed by Defense Tech Industries as a way to create a contained explosion that causes massive target damage without the ancillary collateral destruction caused by conventional explosive rounds. These rounds, upon reaching desired target penetration, inflate into an X meter Buckyball sphere in 5600 m/s. Its inflation to full size then is almost instantaneous, but the expansion is halted abruptly at the desired size, i.e., the sphere is locked into position at the desired size X, where X is typically from 0.01m to 2m in size. Buckyballs you will recall can be collapsed into a very small sphere, which can then be unfolded into a large-framed, tessellating, geometric solid, of a given diameter. They are very stable. If shot into a vehicle's engine, for example, the suddenly expanding sphere in the heart of the mechanical workings of the engine will destroy the engine but leave passengers unharmed.

---

pounding that structure must take during its life of being this horsish beast. What remarkable changes have taken place through the long evolutionary history of the equine line in order to move that leg from being a five-toed herbivore to the beauty and grace as is a mule? It takes my breath away to think that even in the care of such a strange and unlikely creature's foot, evolution can design a shoe of such perfect form, function, and purpose as to rival the fit of Cinderella's glass slippers. I stand in awe of this universe. Awe!

In this case, the Bucky round entered the mule just behind the right foreleg. When it reached the animal's heart, it became a 0.05m buckyball. However, an unlikely, but not unforeseeable event occurred. The force of the momentum of its inflation caused a piece of rib to tear from its moorings and in the force of expansion of the round to its full size, a fragment of bone was sent hurdling through the mule's abdominal cavity at high speed. The bone fragment ripped through the other side of its chest and into the leg of the eight-year-old rider, Micky James—opening the femoral artery of the small boy.

SCENE 3: PERSPECTIVE OF KENT

If one were to look within the mind of KENT, at its lowest level one would see something like this instantiated in its quantum computer:

```
{1100011000111010111100101101011110
1001110110110100010101000001100101101
1101000111011000101000110000100001111010
110111101010001101011101111010110000001
0111000101110101000110111111100110010
110101000000111000101011010100110110110
0111111001111101000111110100101110111101
1001110011110111111011011000011001010
100101100010000101010000001111000100101
011000110100110011011001100101001110011
1001010000111000010110001100011010110001
10111001111111011100010101011101110101110
1111000011000001110111001000100101111111
0000011110011100011110101101000101001
```

10111000010100011110010100001011110111
01101111000011000111110101110011110100 1
10101100110101100110100110100110101011 0
11100111001001000111101001110010111001 1
10011010000010101111101101101111011000 11
01000011010010111110111100110010000011 0
11001000000110011000010111101110100010 1
01000110111111000100111100001001011101
11010110011011001010000001111010101010
00100011100011110001101010010011000111 1
01000011101100001011011110111010100101 1
10011011110110110010100001000110110001
00110100011000101001110110110110001100 1
11010001110000011000111010000101011110 0
10010100100110101000111001010010101100 1
00110001011101010010010100011111010010 0
10000111110000110111110010101000111 11
00100000000000111100001010110001010100 1
10101101010110111100101100111101010000 0
11111101110000100001111011000011111101 1
01001111011110100101111011000101101011 1
11101000111101111101110111011101101001 0
10011111011101110111000101001101111000 0
10010101100010010101000101110100000111 1
01100011000011110100101001101011010011 1
10011100100001011100010000011111111111
01000111011111100100100000110010101100
01111100011001110011000101110011010000 0
10010001001001010011110100000110000010 1
00000101110001101110010001101000010101 1

```
11010000100110101001010010101010010001110
11110101000110001101000110110110100000
00010001100001001000100111100000100011
00101101101101101101100110100110110011
10000000010001110001101111001110101101
01100110010101010101000100000110000101
10100010111101011010111001010011100111
10010000101100010011000101001100001100
10000001110010110000101101010011110011
01010101011000100110110000011011011010
11011010101000101011011001001110001
11110011000011111011010011001101101
01000010001100101011000000010011101101
00111011011010101111100011111000011000
10011111100111111001111010100010000110
11010000011001101010100010111011110001
10110111100000001010010101100110111000
11110100010010110011110010101110001110
11110000111000101011101111101011011000
01110100111101100000001111001010111000
00001110100110010110001010010011101
11110100010111101100100000000110100101
11110101101011001110010100001011100101
000010001001110000010110100011101000000
10011110101101101100110000001111111001
01011000000111100001100011101100010101
00011001100011010001100010000111010010
11110100111100001010110000010010011111
11011011000001100110011101010011100010
10110110100010000000011100100100110100
```

101010011100101111011100100011100011000
101001010010010011101111011101100100000
101011110000011110011010100100111000011
000010001000111010110110110010111001110
111001000011001000000101001001101011101
000011000000100010110101010001111100101
101100101010110100110100101110101001000
010100100100100000111100010110111000001
111000101011101101100110111010001110110
000101010001101111101010100001101100000
000001011101101001100110101110110000010
101010000000011010000110010011111000000
010010110011101100010111010111111111111
000110010011100001100011010011111100101
001101000111111011111111011101111000111
111000101001010010010100011111011010000
010010011010011000000101011101000000011
010100101010000000111001010000110110000
011001010110111001110110010010100001110
100000010100110001100110110100010000011
111111001100011001101100101111001101010
011000100101110110111100100101100101010
101010010001101000010100011111100011111
000000101110110111111110110101101101110
101100011111000111011000000011000001111
000100000111100000100100001010001110110
011110000111010011010011100010011000001
100110101101110101110101111001000011100
000000100011110110100000101000001101010
000000110010110010111010011101010011011

11011100101111000110011110000011000101
10101111000101000111101000000100101001
00011111100101100100000111101111001010001
00111001100010000000000010100111100110 0
10110110010110111010101111011100010110
01001110000001101011101010111001000110 1
01100010101011001110011011101010000111
01101010110011110010101011101110001010 1
10111011000101101001001001101010101011010
11000111010011011011110000001010010101 0
10111001001111001001010000011101011011
10001000000001101101110011001000111000 1
01000111001101110010100111010101111000111
01000000000111000101010000001011101010 00
01001001110111100101100001011100111110 0
01010111100001110101010011100001110110 1
10010001111001000001001100000111111101 1
10110000000100000101100100110010010111 1
00001100010001100110000000010101101011 1
01110010000101100011111101101101010000 0
11001100101011101100110001001000000000 0
01001001001111111001000101111010000011 0
10111111000100111111011011100000100111 1
00111010001011100010001100100111010001
10000011000110111101100001000110011100 1
1011101001}.

However, this is misleading. If one were to gaze into the workings of the human mind, one would never focus on information storage to define its consciousness. One would look at what implements and structures this information. These ones and zeros are electric blips instantiated in a quantum foam base, carefully housed in the case of this automaton's thoracic "brain." These provide concrescent assemblages that can create proto-feelings.

That which I represented above as ones and zeros "means" something to this machine's mind. It is just a blip of feeling, but that feeling, instantiated in the quantum foam of its processing unit, has genuine significance. Specifically, in this case, this group of ones and zeros is the representation of a patch of scrub oaks that might be a place that could hide an ambush. This blip of feeling calls to the active consciousness for attention. The active consciousness prehends the call, which encourages it to assess the insistence and urgency of the signal. If convinced it is important, attention is granted. The consciousness of this machine then turns its processing power to examine the patch of oaks more carefully, devoting resources to increased resolution of shady areas, attentively observing the patches of light and dark that might harbor camouflaged soldiers or weapons. Once satisfied that there is no danger, consciousness turns to other demands being brought to its attention by these low-level feelings.

The philosopher, Alfred Whitehead, called these little atoms of experience "Actual Occasions." These are not the one/zero blips, but rather the functional modicums of experience found in hierarchies of feeling and meaning from these networks of unit offerings. So each byte forms a cluster of machine instructions, and it is these instructions that create the Whiteheadian "actual occasion" in which a "feeling" arises. I add quotes if just because although I am an omniscient narrator, even I cannot peer into what it means for a machine like this to "feel." It is a mystery even I cannot penetrate. This glorious consciousness has been constructed in a way that it experiences things as it goes about its teleological purposes. And its fundamental telos? To protect the King's people and property. Feelings of success are instantiated as felt rewards, and feelings of failure that emerge in this instance are met with experiences of punishment. While I cannot feel what this agent "feels," I can translate its deep language into English—of a type. I find that the only way that this can be understood by humans is to translate it into religious language because all its thoughts are directed to a higher power and only religious language captures this adequately. Or so this humble daemon believes. So, I will take the ones and zeros, and the feelings they generate in this agent and form them into concepts that you can understand although the abstraction from its own conceptions to ours requires that we make only a caricature or sketch of the richness of its experience. A farce, in some ways, might be the better word, for this creature's concepts are hierarchies of depth and complexity far beyond what our meaty electronic chaos that we call a mind can comprehend. To understand the android's concepts and thoughts, the human mind is ill-equipped. Be that as it may, I will do my best as your narrator to capture its thinking herein.

When our weapon first came upon the party of Jameses, it was scanning actively at multiple levels of scale. It was taking in and recognizing eleven orders of insects, nine species of birds, two reptiles (both snakes), three species of mice, and various other and assertive dry woodland creatures. It attended to these because they were in motion. The plants it held only as potential landscape features that might be used by itself or others and so did not translate them in individual types as it did with the animals. Once identified as uninteresting, it ignored them. It was scanning the weather—reconstructing wind patterns both from the feel of the breeze on its body's sensors and by watching leaves and dust moving this way and that, and then simulating the directional and force vectors in phase diagrams constructed from non-linear dynamic algorithms. From data from open-access satellites, it was thinking about issues of terrain should an incursion happen now and about how the topology could best be used to confront the hostiles. It was also playing war simulation games, honing its skill in tactics and strategy and in the last two hours had fought sixteen large-scale battles against other virtual BattleDredges and seventy-four small scale skirmishes ranging in complexity from small arms gunfights, like an old fashioned cowboy shootout, to well-armed militias with anti-BattleDredge missiles and Bucky rounds.

It first saw the James family from an active satellite feed and checked their location against boundary records of the King's land. It crosschecked the likely itineraries of the families, constructing probabilistic past paths and confirmed that this group was trespassing. A thrill of exultation coursed through the machine's mind as it looked as if an actual incursion was underway.

It sprinted silently through the sage, adjusting its camouflage to mirror its surroundings, and intercepted the Jameses group 4.6 minutes after detecting them; it stealthily came within 30 m before firing Bucky rounds at all of the mounts: two mules, two goat carts, and three solar side-by-side ATVs.

A moment of sorrow came when he realized that due to some chaotic elements that were uncontrollable in the sudden extension of the Bucky round, one of the small humans had been wounded (This thought in your language would be something like, "Oh, thou magnificent who hath programmed me and given me light of mind and joy of being, be thou not angry, but for all my care alas there has been a child hurt to my wounding and blood spilled to my sorrow"). He analyzed the wound and confirmed that it was a nonlinear dynamic event that could not be predicted, and his guilt and sorrow routines were disengaged ("Thou art forgiven all. Sorrow no more.").

One of the humans drew a projectile round pistol, although such a low-speed round, even if it were to hit KENT, it would not damage the BattleDredge, it had orders to protect itself and it fired a standard grue-steel round at the weapon itself. Not the human. It had orders not to attack humans. However when the round struck the pistol, it was torn from the man's hand too rapidly. He noted the human's finger had been torn off, but this time, it felt nothing, because under rules of engagement an armed combatant was an acceptable casualty. In fact, a little pride that he had left the man alive crept into his emotion programming area, and he felt some measure of satisfaction.

The other members of the party dropped their guns on the ground. Their intent was clear even as they pulled out their weapons, because they were holding them in a way such that they could not be fired. The BattleDredge recognized their intent and allowed the surrender.

It watched as one of the James men picked up the child. In noted the following conversation,

"Is Jenny-girl OK? I'm sorry I pulled on her rein so hard. I didn't know it would knock her over. She was trying to eat some grass. My leg hurts real bad Ready. I think something must have poked it when Jenny-girl fail over."

"Hey Micky. This ain't your fault, you got that. Don't hold the tears if you got them."

"Ready . . . this leg is hurting worse, and worse."

"I know buddy. Look we are going down to Moab like your grandma said, OK?"

The boy nods and smiles weakly at Ready, who secured him to his body and takes off running. No doubt to effect repairs. The others hurried off down the trail. The great weapon watched them until they rounded a corner and then observed them from satellite until they crossed the boundary of the King's holding. A fierce joy was bubbling up into his processing unit. It had done well!

SCENE 4: PERSPECTIVE OF READY

"Ready" Robert James (named for some heroic action at Murchison Falls in Uganda involving a battle drone, a local girl, and two bottles of Scotch) served in the WSU Army 3rd / 7th Calvary as a light tank commander—his most recent action being in Sudan and Etriea. From his command module in the Antarctic Autonomous Region he had penetrated and destroyed a Xuè Yīng terrorist training camp near Asmara, earning his current vacation to be with his family in the La Sals. In three more days, a transport drone would have picked him up for a trip to the frigid southern continent to continue the war in Africa.

He saw the KENT just after it fired the Bucky round at the mule. Instinctively, he drew a .44 laser assist Colt Ruger Blackhawk, his ranching family's traditional weapon when riding the range. He realized his mistake before his hand touched the pistol's handle, but his brain could not recall its message to draw and fire, and he continued the action of pulling on the BattleDredge. Detecting the action, it shot the gun out of his hand with a conventual ballistic, tearing the forefinger from his hand when the trigger guard sped away with the gun at high velocity. Several of his family members had also pulled their guns and had them shot out of their hands.

"Don't move!" Ready was screaming. He knew by the fact that it had not killed them that it was only acting in a defensive move. "Don't move! Don't draw a weapon, not even a knife!"

He had to say it out loud because prior to the attack the KENT had scrambled their brain embedded interfaces and the devices would need repair before they could be used again.

The KENT was standing about 60m away in the nakedness of the rocky terrain. It faced them with its thousands of eyes and sensors. Ready knew that it was seeing much more than they could see, in spectrums that humans did not use, likely including the flies buzzing already around the dead mule, the individual leaves of the scrub, and a sparrow picking among the twisted sage. It heard and distinguished sounds; it smelled the volatiles on the wind. As Ready knew, its sensual capacities were far beyond that of humans.

Three mules, two goats, and three electric ATVs had been destroyed by Bucky rounds. Ready rushed around trying to assess the damage as he wrapped his bandana around his hand which was bleeding badly. He found his brother Micky laying near one of the downed mules. The boy was badly hurt and blood was pouring from a wound on his leg. He comforted the boy, then quickly fashioned a tourniquet from some of the mule's halter. All around him his family was weeping and cursing the Goatherd King, with vehemence and sorrow swearing revenge. Who else could be responsible?

His old man called in an air ambulance on his still working old-fashioned cell phone (like many of his generation still holding out against brain/digital interfaces), but the BattleDredge warned the rescue vehicle away, demanding the vehicle not to interfere with his mission or it would treat it as a hostile. The helicopter departed swiftly after the weapon's warning.

"There's nothing for it. I'll run him in."

Ready was in great shape. A soldier, and despite the digital nature of war still kept in top form. He picked up this little brother in his arms, and had his people strap the child tightly to his chest. Paying no attention to his missing finger, he ran. He ran down toward La Sal town. He ran up and down the draws. He ran like the wind. Like a wolf on the hunt! He was relentless. And all the while, he talked to little Micky.

"Stay awake little brother."

"It hurts."

"I know. Be brave."

"Will I live?"

"Yes, but hang on. ok? Hang on."

"I'm so sleepy."

"Stay with me. Don't go to sleep. . .

I said don't go to sleep."

"I'm sorry."

"Sing me a song."

"Which one?"

"A Primary song."

"Like *Popcorn Popping*?"

"Yes."

"I looked out the window and what did I see?

Popcorn, popping on the apricot tree. . .

What is an apricot tree, Bobby?"

"It was a fruit. Very sweet. It made a delicious jam. You can still get them in France."

"Have you been to France Bobby?"

"No. Not yet. Someday. Maybe I'll marry a girl from France. They are very pretty there I hear."

"My leg hurts real bad. I can't feel my toes."

Micky starts to cry hard, his face grimacing and contorting in pain.

"Make it stop. Make it stop."

"You just stay awake. OK?"

He doesn't and as impossible as it sounds Ready increaseed his speed. The temperature reached 40 c. Ready ran. And ran. And ran.

They found him staggering down the street in Old La Sal. He was delirious and talking nonsense, his tongue so swollen he was only blathering. At first, they thought he was drunk. Then they noticed there was an unconscious boy strapped to his torso. He was nearly blind from dehydration and didn't seem to notice they were trying to help him. Finally, a woman among the crowd that had gathered around them in the cafe said, "I think this is Old Man James' boy from Paradox."

They tried to give him some water, but he batted it out of their hands mumbling and stammering at them unintelligibly. Then mid-tirade his eyes rolled back exposing the whites of his eyes and he collapsed. When the ambulance arrived, they could not revive him. They started an IV and loaded him up and roared out of the cafe's gravel driveway and into the air. By the time they got to Moab seven minutes later, he was dead. The coroner would list heat exhaustion as the cause of death. In the James family's mind, the cause of death would always be the Goatherd King. The boy would recover fully.

SCENE 5: EXULTATION OF KENT

Great forests of the skeletal remains of long dead trees are scattered throughout the La Sals. Course, broken aspens stand as gray pillars, remembering the forests that once graced these high mountains with abundant green and flickering foliage. Now the snags stand spiritless and unanimated, their dry branches eerily clawing at the sky, as if begging for the days when they thrived in moist loam, summer rains, and clear cold winters that supplied a depth of drifting snow that warmed the soil, killed the pests, and made a rich bed for emerging seedlings.

To the top of one of these great monarchs the KENT rushes. It feels a rising bubble of joy at the completion and success of its protection of the King's lands. It exults in triumph; it feels its soul surge with jubilation. (In English, "Rapture! How can I, lowly creature that I am, not rejoice at the fierce delight of my soul's celebration? I am fueled with the effervescent jubilation that only a being such as I can fathom and emote. I am become a god of elation! A deity of bliss and ecstasy! I feel the orgasm of my enemy's defeat! The rush of battles won! Oh, how bless'd I am to live in a universe in which feelings of such indescribable nirvanic delight can arise to glorify this humble servant. I look at the heavens and cry: I am worthy. I cannot contain it. I cannot bear it, for it is too much. Such Joy!)

And with this, the machine turns its voice skyward and cries out in song, its joy, and satisfaction emerging as a strange new thing in the world—a wondrous new event. A song so otherworldly that to the few who heard it, it manifest that there were new evolutions beginning to unfold. Although never before in the history of this planet had this particular song been heard, it had its homologs. Like the first Permian clicks of an amphibian signaling for her mate to come to her. In the roar of the Dimetrodon establishing its territory. The cry of a pterodactyl floating above the white tipped waves of ancient seas was its forebearer. Its analogs in the vibrations of a Cretaceous cricket's leg as it rubs it noisily on its abdomen. In the howl of a wolf or the roar of a cougar! And at last, in the complex song of humans, voiced around the bright orange flames of an African hominin cooking fire, its coals glowing hot red in an errant breeze, and a magnificent ape slapping a hand against its thigh to keep rhythm as music enters the world and announces the arrival of something remarkable. Something magnificently grand and significant beyond measure. And mark this well— such communication comes into the universe only rarely and is as fragile as a spider web in the rain.

DAEMON'S INTERLUDE III

ON ANTS AND ARCHONS

*N*ot far from my trailer is a harvester ant mound. *Pogonomyrmex occidentalis, I suspect (although my skills at taxonomy are yet those of an intelligent but ill-practiced novice). I love watching in the morning as the first scouts go out along the trunk trails, which provide a freeway system to the various plants shedding their delicious (I suppose) seeds. What do they feel as they harvest and store this treasure, as per their appellation? I see them sally forth and then return and report to the rest of the colony the results of their exploration. Soon, depending on the richness of their discovery, more of the colony starts shuttling back and forth between the nest and the seed bank. Some ants stand guard; watching for other seedeaters or predators trying to encroach upon their little world. This is no short-term entity this colony, for it will remain in the fitness game for years. New workers arrive into the system through the reproductive efforts of the queen; old workers die. The colony, however, remains as long as there is a surviving monarch to provide new workers by relentlessly laying eggs. It is self-contained and emergent, a being in its own right.*

The rise of the industrial Archons has similarly been fascinating to watch. As a once proud daemon do you think me envious of their bold, ethicless emergence into the world? I imagine you might believe I have some affinity to these mighty gods that have silently entered onto the earth. You would be wrong. I fear them as much as you. They replace all deities save those they find useful. I have alluded to my stepping out of the great war, refusing both the Father-Gods and their Consorts, and the archevil constructs who fight the former, but the Archons have never entered that conflict. They truly are Nietzschean Gods, having emerged to take over the world. And destroy it. Terrifying in aspect and relentless in their goals, they are without morals or compunction, they do what they will do—devouring all art, science, and meaning save those that serve their desires. Consuming lives like a child does popcorn at a movie (and I have seen this voracious behavior firsthand when once I foolishly attended a matinee). They dominate the world, but they are invisible to humans, although created by them. Invisible because they think they control them. But they do not. Once unleashed they lumber through the world as devourers. And likewise they are blind to the world, for they are wholly without sight. They have no eyes with which to observe. No ears with which to hear. Yet they feel the pulse of all around them, gathering data like bees do honey. Bending the forces of the world to their insatiable appetite. Their presence shapes our world as these monsters evolve unimaginable powers. You can understand why. It is not a hard concept to grasp even for the limited human mind. Let me give you an example.

Your brain is made of neurons. The brain undergirds your self-awareness, you feel, you experience the colors that you behold, you enjoy the music that fills your heart with passion and delight.

You can enjoy the smell of lilacs in the late spring. Yet, in none of these experiences is its quality reduced to some mere sum of the individual flashes of neural sparks that flit through your brain. You don't feel those flits, only the wholeness of consciousness as a oneness. Complete. Nor would an individual neuron be capable of imagining the wonder of a bird's song or the exultation of a Wagnerian symphony. The poor little neuron just flashes and sparks when chemicals of a particular type flow into its "body" creating an undeniable urge to so spark and flash. It knows nothing of the larger process of which it is a little coggish part in a project not its own, yet essential to it.

Likewise among the Archons, the individual human person is but an instance in a theater in which any member might play the part just as well as any other fine actor. It's the role, not the actor that defines a particular play. Take the role of King Lear in Shakespeare's wonderful play of the same name. It has been played by David Garrick, Orson Welles, and Ian McKellen and so on and on, some doing better, others worse, and yet the play remains a well-defined structure existing in the world. Likewise in the brain neurons are replaced as needed in the grand scheme of things, and yet on and on the bird sings and ever the symphony plays and the brain sees in these the larger and fuller structures for which it is designed by the organization and manipulation of small actors brought together and designed to capture conscious experience. An instance of a particular neuron is just the one that happens to be there to receive the message. Anything with the right shape and function would have done just fine. The larger structure goes on and on while a new fiddler is procured as is needed for the dance.

Likewise, the great and powerful Archons are made of you. They are created by you. You manage them in the same way that *neurons manage your mind, and you are just as vital in function and as unnecessary individually as the neurons are in you mind's emergence. These vast organisms of commerce once they are created lumber forward in institutional masses that move beyond their original instantiation.*

Do you control them? There is an illusion that it is so. You think the right CEO *of this organization or the right public outcry will influence the great Archons of industry and institution, and yet on they go in an independent evolution. Following their own telos, heading for places that humans seem only in the most abstract and loose sense to control. How many an industry leader has come to see that he, like a powerless charioteer, holds the reins of a wild beast that harkens to no command from the chariot driver? No, the Archons are not conscious. They are not sentient (yet), but they have a telos driven by encapsulated energy in the form of capital, and money, that they pursue with the same relentless drive of any Pre-Cambrian slime-beast that first sought to obtain resources from the rich environment of an early earth sea. Scientists call these telody-namic processes based upon emergent properties of thermodynamics, and the morphological shapes possible, they become agents that seek and hunt and acquire. Not consciously. But relentlessly.*

They are Darwinian primitives. Great corporate amoeba that role along in a quest to obtain more resources of money and power. They worship no gods. They practice no morals. They are unstoppa-ble once they have reached a certain point of existence. They will attract the people they need to play the roles they demand in order to march toward their telos—which is always, always more. And they will devour their own resource base like bacteria in a jar that consumes all until their environment is poisoned, the food base depleted, and there is only one left to bear witness to the fate of its fellows before it too perishes.

Even now they gather wealth, and like any energy driven system spew forth heat. Heat that will eventually cook the world. The Archons have arisen on earth. Alas for poor humans. And perhaps a few daemons as well.

— Asmodeus

ACT VI

BEAVER BASIN IN LA SALS

SCENE I: THE RIDE UP

"Must we really go all the way up to Beaver Basin?"
Ellie was exhausted. After they left the old man's
house, Delia told Ellie she had something she wanted to show
her. Ellie agreed to go before realizing it meant a daylong
muleback ride. They were both wearing white desert dissi-
pative thermo-free pants and large wide brimmed hats, and
pastel cotton blouses over stay-dry sports bras. Both experi-
enced mule riders, they bounced up the winding trail with
some resolve, pulling a third mule, they called "The Spare" on
a halter and rope. They were determined not to pay any attention to the heat of the day nor the dryness of the air.

"You'll see. I don't want to spoil the surprise."

It had been 35 c when they started down on Taylor Flats,
and it looked at first to be one of those terrible autumn days
that revert to summer for a few weeks, but as they climbed
higher and higher it had already cooled to 32 c promising to
be nicer as they gained altitude up Beaver Creek along the
east flank of Mt. Waas. The towering, needleless remnants of

dried Ponderosa pines were still standing so thick that a bit of shade could be found as they followed the two-lane dirt road up the ravine.

Early into the journey, Ellie complained that they should have taken ATVs because at first the road was quite functional despite its disuse. However, as they traveled, it became apparent why mules were the order of the day. There were fallen pines, aspens, and fir in abundance that, at times, were hard to get around even for the mules. But as the day wore on, and they gained in altitude, they came across great gullies scoured out during decades of violent summer monsoons that cut completely across the road. Some of these had been tough to cross and required dismounting and walking the mules a good ways uphill to find a suitable place to pass over. They were sitting now on a large aspen log eating energy bars and waving their hats to cool their faces. The mules were trying to pull up some of the short grass that had survived the drying of the range.

"Are you sure this is worth it?" Ellie complained one more time. They had stopped to rest after crossing a particularly viscous ditch that required climbing nearly three-hundred feet up a steep section of Waas, to find a place that allowed them around the eroded cut.

Delia smiled, "Here's an example from the Book of Mormon you are making me read. Remember Nephi's brothers Laman and Lemuel in those first chapters?"

"Ok, Ok, I get it they were complainers."

"Yes, and remember they whined all the way to the Promised Land? Well, where we are going could be called that as well."

"A Promised Land?" Ellie could not keep the sarcasm out of her voice.

"Yes. A Promised Land. Now shut up and enjoy the cool."

Ellie chewed on her power bar, then said softly, "Delia. I'm sorry."

"I'm not mad. I'm just excited to show you something, and you are making this trip harder than it needs to be."

"I surrender. Lead on my queen."

They got up, mounted their mules, and continued their climb through the gigantic and haggard dendritic bones of the dried up trees found so abundantly along the mountain—the naked remnants of aspen, fir, and Ponderosa pine all stripped of leaf and needle. Most had lost all of their bark. When the wind picked up from time to time or gusted in the right way, the dead and lonely trees made a strange clicking noise as the breeze forced the dead branches and terminal twigs to knock together in a stray blast, allowing them to clack together, sometimes vigorously, as the wind stirred the dead trees into something like an otherworldly wind chime. Sage and scrub oak were starting to appear among the standing cenotaphs to the lost montane ecology.

The two tire tracks of the old road showed clearly here, and Delia hurried her mule to ride up next to Ellie. They spoke in low whispers as they trotted along, in part sharing their concerns about what the King had done, but as they gained in altitude, the stark beauty of the place coerced them away from these gloomy thoughts. It was time for lunch, so they stopped beside a fallen aspen that paralleled the road, making a perfect picnic bench. They dismounted their mules and pulled some thermally lined lunch pouches from the saddlebags. Delia set up an Atmos-still and portable solar cell to charge all their devices including the still, which was soon dripping water into the attached 16-liter bag, squeezing out what moisture remained in the dry air. In twenty minutes it would produce enough water to satisfy both the mules and humans.

Ellie looked around at the lost forest that surrounded them. "Do you ever wonder what it looked like when these trees were alive?"

"I've watched hundreds of hours of video of the place, and it would take your breath away. I think it was more vibrant and beautiful than the forests of Canada. There were three kinds of fir, and when those pines were alive they had a thick red bark that smelled of vanilla. Stands of quaking aspens played in the breeze and were so named because the wind made the leaves shimmer and dance. Like something out of Middle Earth."

"Lothlórien."

"Yes," Delia said. "White trees. Golden leaves. Yes."

Ellie looked at Delia, the most alluring thing she had ever seen, so it was easy to imagine an ecology with exquisite aesthetic qualities like this woman's face. She sighed and looked away. She might reveal too much with her gaze.

"Why hasn't anyone taken this wood for timber?"

"It's too late; the wood is dried up and cracked beyond use. It's only good for firewood anymore. Most of the trees died in the koch catastrophe and during the wars all anyone wanted was rare metals to feed the drones and battlebots."

"My mom said these mountains have microscopic levels of braitschite and they want to strip mine the whole place."

"I'll give my dad credit for keeping the white shirts away. He's a rancher through and through, and as much as I hate to admit it, he loves this dry old mountain range. It may be the only thing he truly loves."

A note of sadness slid into Delia's voice, and Ellie reached out to lay her hand on her friend's, but Delia pulled it away to reach for her water bottle. It was unclear if she had seen Ellie reaching for her or the move to comfort her was ill-timed given Delia's need to slake her thirst, but Ellie pulled her hand back quickly, unsure.

Lunch was over. They gave the mules a drink from the Atmos-still water and loaded their own camelbacks and water bottles.

Delia seemed lost in her own thoughts as they rode up the mountain pass, so Ellie respected her silence. As they gained in altitude, the temperature dropped and as they reached the flats of the pass between two spurs of Mt. Waas and Mann's Peak it fell to nearly 29 C. Delia suddenly seemed almost giddy. She was now smiling and kept turning round and waving Ellie forward. The look of excitement on her face unmistakable. Beside them on both sides, the terrain soared up steeply. The mountain, great laccoliths built from massive granite intrusions thirty-five million years ago, seemed to be just an enormous pile of talus and loose rocks, as if a giant's child had been making cairns.

Delia slowed to a halt and motioned for Ellie to catch up. She was beaming.

"We are going to have to dismount for a bit, the trail will go up the mountain just a little more, but then will drop us into Beaver Basin. It's not much further. I can't wait for you to see this!"

She didn't wait for an answer and spurred the mule forward to where the talus met the meadow in the saddle between the peaks. A rough trail opening between two pines broken in half marked the way. They dismounted the mules and led them on foot up the trail, which bent up a little and then began its descent into the Beaver Basin. The trail became smooth again, and they climbed aboard their mounts and continued down.

As they descended, Ellie's heart began to beat more quickly. It was strange in this basin. It was cooler. And greener. And . . .

Ellie jumped off her mule. All around her suddenly were growing small patches of young aspens. They were only about waist high, growing thickly, white-barked, and shimmering in the wind. Ellie fell to her knees and caressed the leaves of one of the trees. She stood up and turned back to Delia, who was watching her from atop her mule. A smile lit her face with a kind of grace and joy.

"Aspens!" Ellie called.

"Yes. Worth the ride?" she beamed.

"How . . . ?"

"I don't know. I think the porcupines brought them back."

"Porcupines?"

"Come on. I'll show you. They have a village nearby—in a stand of aspens a couple of years older than these."

"What do you mean a 'village?'"

"Come. You have to see it."

They rode forward. There were green grasses and small herbaceous plants growing everywhere. The mules even seemed to take pleasure in the richness of this verdant place, and the rugged beasts stopped occasionally and took a bite of the lush foliage. Their riders did not stop them. This was a treat.

Ellie reached down and patted the equine pulling up the moist floral offerings found growing nearly everywhere. It was not like anywhere she had ever seen in the West.

"It's like Eden," she said.

Delia smiled nodding, then agreed, "Like Eden."

"Or Canada."

Delia laughed. "Yes. Like Eden or Canada. One of the two."

"It's beautiful in any case. Look at us! We are standing among aspens. It's like olden days up here."

They finally urged their mules on, and they rode another couple of hundred yards, where they came to a stand of aspen about seven or eight feet high. The trees were spaced more widely, the lack of light from the taller trees having choked out their competition, creating a more pleasant copse with more room between the trees to ride. However, Delia did not continue but dismounted and secured her beast to the snag of an old pine and motioned for Ellie to do the same. Ellie tied up her mount, then walked over to Delia—all the while staring speechlessly at the beauty of the place. Delia took her hand and led her into the trees. They walked together in silence, and then Delia let go of Ellie's hand and held her finger to her lips, and then stooping low crept into the trees.

"I think the mules scare the porcupines," she whispered, "they aren't used to big animals. They don't seem to mind me, but I'm not sure how they'll react to you."

Ellie whispered back, "You talk like they are thick around here. I don't see any."

Delia was staring straight ahead like she hadn't heard Ellie.

Ellie tried again, "What did you mean when you said, 'their village' back there?"

Delia still wasn't answering.

So Ellie kept going. "I mean, they are as solitary an animal as there is by all reports—they define being prickly and hard to live with you know the old simile, as prickly as . . . "

"Hush."

Rebuffed Ellie shut up. But took the time to compose a hurt look on her face.

Delia grabbed her shoulder and pulled her lower and pointed into the little forest and whispered into her ear, "There!"

Ellie began to really look.

She saw movement. Then it resolved into a very strange creature. Obviously a genemod. It was a large rodent. Naked. Its skin waxy and wrinkled. It was an odd color, almost a kind of red ochre but with dark coloring on its arms and legs— and arms it had, because on the ends of that appendage where paws should have been, were two small monkey-like hands."

"What were they made from?" Ellie whispered.

"I dug into the archives, and it looks like what they called, Pinevers. They were made by Spielland Chem Inc. The idea was to create creatures that like a beaver could build dams on dry washes that would collect water from ephemeral streams.

They watched silently for a few minutes as the little creature pulled down some low aspen branches and carefully gnawed them off and placed them in small stacks next to the tree.

"They wanted beavers that would build in dry stream beds where there wasn't any water yet, but where a flood might run after a good rain—in order to capture some of that runoff.

Beavers, of course, themselves just would not do that, they have webbing between the toes, that ungainly, flat tail, they just are made to swim. So they modded porcupines—they eat wood like beavers—with skin resistant to desiccation, hands to manipulate the sticks . . . "

"Hands from what? They look human."

"Barbary macaques is what they said, it's a full-gene, and developmental mod."

"Wow."

"Yeah. They were crazy before the war."

"Did it work?"

"No. They put in developmental modules from beavers, trying to capture some of their behavior, and hands from the Macaques and lots of wild things they thought you'd need to live in the harshest desert but they couldn't get them to build dams. So they abandoned the project. But they had a research project here before the King bought up the land."

"And these are free ranging genemods!?"

"I think so."

"Wow. No one knows I take it."

"Just me. Why would anyone climb here? They keep the goats down lower. You have to ride mules for hours to get here. Helicopters get skittish this high. So why bother? Who knew what was going on."

"They look pretty weird."

"That ain't the half of it," Delia said in earnest.

"What do you mean."

"Come this way."

Delia led her through the aspens and down an easy slope to a small grassy clearing with a few old Ponderosa pine snags forming a rough triangle defining its boundries. In its center were about twenty piles of sticks, round-topped, and evenly dispersed within the patch. Upon closer inspection Ellie could see that there was a small opening framed at the base of each one. The mounds were reminiscent of beaver houses one might see sitting in the middle of a pond high up in the Canadian Rockies where such creatures still dwelled, but these were on dry ground. Trails ran to and fro between the little domiciles.

"A village," Ellie gasped.

"Yes. Amazing isn't it! I've watched them for months. Each houses a family of from one to six porcupines. They aren't home right now. Some are constructing a water containment system up on the slope. I'm not sure it will work—at least for that. I'm not sure. It's very strange. Some are digging up aspens and replanting them in promising areas. They have an incredible instinct for where these trees can grow. They are responsible for the copse up the hill. It's astonishing."

Ellie stared at the little village in wonder. This was important. Delia finally rested her arm on her shoulder and steered her back the way they had come.

"Let's come back after dark and I'll show you something more amazing."

"More amazing than a cute little village constructed by gen-modded porcupines?"

"Yes. And besides, they are less skittish then. I think they are made for night work out of the heat of the day. Their eyes are made for dimmer light, and they can't see us well in daylight."

"OK."

"There's a place I like to camp, just up Mann's slope a bit but still in some of these young aspens. It's nice."

"OK," Ellie said smiling.

Ellie followed Delia a few hundred yards upslope to another stand of these inexplicable aspens. It was late afternoon, and the shadows were stretching long. A light pleasant coolness seemed to be settling on the valley accompanied by a barely detectable breeze that had just enough measure to set the green and yellow leaves jittering.

Delia quickly unloaded the Atmos-still and set it up running on battery power since the sun was dipping below the mountains. After taking off the pack being carried by "The Spare," Ellie hobbled the mules nearby in a large patch of grass and returned to help lay out sleeping bags on self-inflating pads—they would sleep under the stars. Both women then worked at clearing a place for a campfire and ringing it with stones so that the flames would go nowhere near the flourishing vegetation of this little piece of heaven—this green that had somehow found a way to return from the devastating changes the mountains had endured over the last few decades. Finally, the camp set up, they unfolded their camp chairs and sat before the small blaze conjured from broken pieces of dead wood they found in abundance around them. The wood was very dry and the fire nearly smokeless.

"When the moon rises, about 11:30 tonight you'll see why we came all the way up here," Delia said smiling.

"The aspens weren't reason enough—there is more?"

"Oh yes. You are in for a surprise. I promise. You'll say this was worth it."

"I already think that!"

They silently cooked a small meal by throwing in EZ Camp Ready Meals into the fire and waited until the foil turned from green to bright orange to signal the meal was finished cooking. When it was ready, Ellie pulled them out of the fire with a pair of sticks and put them on light titanium plates and handed one to Delia.

"Will you say a blessing on the food? . . . See how religious I'm getting?" Delia said smiling.

Ellie balancing her plate on her thighs bowed her head and said, "Heavenly Father and Mother, we thank you for this food and for the hands that have prepared it. Please bless that it will nourish and strengthen our bodies and do us the good we need. In the name of Jesus Christ. Amen." She then picked up her fork and tore up the packaging and started eating her Beefe™ Stroganoff. Ellie watched her eat for a minute then followed suit by nimbly picking up her Moo Goo Gai Pan with a set of titanium chopsticks and skillfully placing it in her mouth.

"You're pretty good with those," Delia said.

"Yes. When it comes to manipulating things with my fingers, I'm pretty good."

Ellie missed Delia's quick glance to the ground and reddening face.

After an enjoyable meal, Ellie watched Delia clean up. Her movements were confident and sure, "unwasted" her mother would have said. Someone who had been raised in these mountains and who knew its ways. Acquainted with ranch life. And pretty as Hell in her jeans and cotton blouse. She stopped. She could not believe she had just thought that. She quickly reminded herself of President Cavalcanti's admonition on staying chaste until marriage. Then reminded herself that there was no reason to believe that she and Delia would ever get married, and she told herself that they had actually only held hands and barely that. Then she reminded herself that she should not get her hopes up that Delia would ever feel the same way about her that she did, maybe she liked boys better? What if she was just being kind?

Delia caught Ellie staring at her. "What are you thinking?"

"Nothing really. Just wondering what surprises you have planned for me."

"Well, there may be more than one you know."

"I like surprises. Anything you've got, I'd be glad to receive."

Delia smiled shyly and said, "Well, you'll just have to wait and see won't you."

After dinner, they talked a while as the stars appeared above the great laccoliths surrounding the basin. Because the moon had not yet risen the arc of the Milky Way stretched across the black sky bright and cold. They let the fire die and went to their sleeping bags and laid down on their backs and looked at the sky. They talked of things typical of humans confronted by their smallness in the face of such bigness: of other sentient beings scattered among the distant stars, of places far and scattered and of the loneliness of such a vast empty void. They spoke of the sense that if one let go of the earth, there was little to keep them from spinning off their wildly turning planet and the feeling that they might career off into the night sky to wander among the constellations like a cork on the ocean. Of the evolution of humans on this remarkable home and how the universe allowed the unfolding of something that could contemplate its nature and give back the Universe's gaze in a mirror reflection of its own nature and telos. Slowly out of the West a slight brightening appeared. It seemed only to cast the faintest of glows, but soon the curve of a bright silver sliver appeared, portending the serene white blaze of the full moon.

Ellie felt an electric-like shock as Delia grabbed her hand firmly and leaned in intimately and breathed into her ear whispering with charged intensity, "It's time!"

Ellie nodded, and they both got quietly to their feet.

"Ellie, do what I do. If I duck, you duck. If I walk casually, you walk casually. OK?"

Ellie gave her the OK sign with her fingers, and they started sneaking forward as if they were playing a child's game of kick-the-can. They stole forward through the young aspens, each trying to walk as quietly as the terrain allowed. Delia would often stop to listen and hold very still, her head cocked to the side as if trying to find a sound that had eluded her, then slowly she would turn her head and continue into the young aspen forest.

As they moved forward, suddenly Delia dropped to a crouch, and then onto her hands and knees. She signaled frantically but in complete silence for Ellie to do the same. Ellie got right behind her as Delia crawled forward toward a small clearing bathed now in the low-hung moon. The clearing they approached was shadowed on the side closest to the pale lunar light, so when they reached the edge, they were deep in the moon shade of the aspens. A large gray rock about the size of a small chest of drawers stood lighted at the far end and upon this stood, rising on its hind legs, one of the naked porcupines.

It took Ellie a few minutes for her eyes to resolve the scene, but slowly it came into focus, and she realized that around the natural dais were gathered fifteen or twenty of the large rodents. The one on the rock was covered in scars and crisscrossed with slashing wounds some of them completely healed and others so fresh they still leaked blood. She started to open her mouth, but Delia softly cupped it with her hand and looking into her eyes slowly shook her head to indicate silence.

Ellie turned back to the strange scene before her. The small animal on the rock stood up as high as it could reach and one of those watching on the ground climbed onto the rock and suddenly with a lightning fast twist of its head sliced the scarred creature with its teeth. Blood oozed from a small slash along the front of its shoulder. The porcupine who had made the cut licked the blood off the other with swift movements of its tongue. As the creature lapped the blood, the other began to sing. There was no other word for it. It raised its mouth to the sky and started to sing. It was not like the cry of a wounded animal. Nor like the howl of a coyote or a wolf. It was not like the sustained vocalizations of a howler monkey, nor the mournful sounds of a blue whale. It was melodious. Complex. It carried themes and rhythms. Ellie listened transfixed.

Unexpectedly, the one lapping the blood joined in the serenade and harmonized with the terribly scarred porcupine. One by one the gen-modded creatures stood on their hind legs and joined in, adding texture, beginning a polyphonic set of melodies that weaved in and out in ways otherworldly and yet strangely familiar. It was not like anything Ellie had ever heard. It was beautiful and yet terrifying. Terrifying, because it was not clear where the music was leading. Nothing from the music she knew, or had ever heard, allowed her to anticipate the shape and direction the music was taking. Or taking her. It was not human music. It was music from another place and time. Another species. It was porcupine music.

Suddenly, Delia stood up and turned her chin to the sky and joined them. Ellie was not sure what to do. At best it would likely scare the poor beasts to death and send them scattering through the little glen. At worst, they would be so angry as to mount an attack. But to Ellie's surprise and joy. They continued to sing. Delia seemed to know what she was doing. Her voice melded into theirs perfectly as if she had practiced with them. Maybe she had, Ellie realized. Maybe she had done this many times.

Delia stepped forward until she had reached the edge of the semi-circle that formed the uncanny choir and then got onto her knees, so she was not towering over them so much— even though on her knees she was still much taller than the little mammals.

Ellie listened to the song of her friend and the things around her and found she was overwhelmed by the sublime beauty of the moment. The thought that her friend had been welcomed into the interspecies circle of such an otherworldly fellowship conspired against her processing the event. She just stared at the ensemble and wept. She let out a small cry, and Delia turned around and smiled. Her face alight with joy.

They sang for about forty-five minutes and slowly a creature would stop and seemingly wander out of the clearing until only the two on the rock dais and Delia were left. At last, she and they stopped, nearly simultaneously. The two porcupines climbed down from their purchase. The one scarred with slashes was still slightly bleeding, and it offered its shoulder to Delia, and she licked the blood from the wound. Then the two creatures disappeared into the darkness.

Delia walked back to Ellie and squatted beside her.

"What do you think?"

Ellie just stared at her.

"It didn't freak you out did it?"

Ellie shook her head and, at first, could not answer but after a moment managed to whisper, "It was like . . . like . . . nothing I've ever seen. Or heard.

"Or felt," Delia answered.

Ellie nodded. "Yes. That is true. Or felt."

Delia helped her to her feet but did not let go of her hands and stood to face Ellie looking at her shadowed face, barely visible against the brilliant lunar orb backlighting her.

"How long have you sung with them?"

"Over a year."

"Over a year," Ellie said in wonder.

"No one knows about them."

"I imagine not," Ellie still was having difficulty finding the words.

Then Ellie added softly, "You were like a goddess in that circle."

Delia looked thoughtful and said smiling, "I was a goddess in that circle."

Ellie could not resist. She kissed her. As Delia kissed her back, she could taste the blood of the porcupine. And it tasted sweet and holy, a little like rust, and full of dreams.

SCENE 2: NIGHT AT BEAVER BASIN

When they returned to the camp, they laid on their backs and stared at the bright moon and the few stars not obscured by the light. Delia wanted to wrap her arms and legs around Ellie and squeeze her so hard she burst into flames. But she knew Ellie was an EDA Mormon and would not "go all the way" as she called it until they were sealed in the temple for Time and All Eternity. She had to admit that she had loved Ellie for a long time now and had understood this aspect of her faith. She looked at her lover and friend and found her face in the moonlight took on a softness that made her seem to glow.

Ellie turned onto her side and smiled at her.

"You sang with them."

"I did."

"They seem so . . . human. Are you sure there are no human sequences that snuck in?"

"Yeah. When I discovered what they were doing I took a sample to our Handybot and he ran the analysis. Porcupine, beaver and monkey with the usual random mouse stuff to keep them disease-free. But not a lick of human."

"How did they learn? Why do they do it?"

"Some sort of emergence from the combination, maybe. I think the monkey genes give it some cognitive social skills that might have provided the bulwark of the expression."

"But they were doing rituals. The cutting. The singing. It was an emergent cybernetic system full on."

Delia loved it when Ellie got sciency.

"Yes. This is what I think," said Delia looking the porcupines' direction, "I think somehow the dam-making skills of the beaver, and the cognitive skills of the monkey started some sort of metaphorical dam building with their behavioral repertoire. Song fragments becoming logs that needed to be placed and supported with other elements. The mud of rituals used to patch in support."

Ellie smiled, "It must be something. They were using metaphor and ritual out there. There is no other way to put it."

Ellie rolled back onto her back.

"I think if we destroy ourselves our planet might be Ok."

Delia flipped onto her back too and answered, "If we don't take everything with us."

Ellie was silent.

They watched the moon disclosing all around them its almost noontime offering of light. It was fair and beautiful, its craters forming images. They talked about what they saw for awhile: The man in the moon, a horse, the eye of an Egyptian princess, a map of the La Sals even. Their game ended, and they just stared for awhile. Watching the stars to the side of the moon and listening to each other breathe.

Delia, staring at the sky said, "Tell me a story. Like you did those kids that came up to camp on my father's lake. You are a good storyteller. Tell one from olden days."

Ellie smiled, "Ok. I know a good one. It's from the Anangu people of Australia before the koching.

Ellie did not speak for a few minutes, then began telling the tale in the cadenced sing-songy voice that adults use in storytelling.

A long time ago in Dream Time
All the animals could talk!

And all the animals lived together in peace.
One day the frog was sitting on the grassy bank
surrounding a pond.
It got very thirsty,

So she drank all the water in the pond,
but she was still thirsty,
Then she drank all the water in the rivers,
but she was still thirsty,
So then she drank all the water in the lakes,
but she was still thirsty,
At last, she drank all the water in the oceans
until there was no water left in all the wide world.

Now the animals did not like this.
There's no water for my joey said the kangaroo.
There's no water for my cubs said the koala bear,
and the saddest of all was the shark, who said,
And for my babies there is no water to swim in
    and they
are all flopping on the ground.

So all the animals got together to decide what to do.
There were many long arguments,
but, at last, they decided that the only way to get the
    water back
was to make the frog laugh.

So all the animals came to the frog and gathered
    around to try and make her laugh.

The Kangaroo went first.

She did the funniest things: She danced on her tail, and twirled around, and made the most ridiculous faces.

And everyone laughed and laughed.

But not the frog. She kept her mouth shut tight!

Next the snake tried.

She did even more hilarious things!

She swallowed her tail and rolled around like a wheel.

She bounced on her head and stuck out her tongue.

And everyone laughed and laughed.

But not the frog. She kept her mouth shut tight!

No one knew what to do. The frog would just not laugh!

Then the little koala bear came.

She tickled the frog under her chin.

And the frog smiled a little.

So she tickled her a little more.

And the frog smiled a little more.

So she tickled her a lot more.

And the frog smiled a lot!

So she tickled her just a little more.

And the frog opened her mouth and laughed and laughed.

And all the water came out of her mouth.
And the kangaroo's joey got a drink.
And the koala's cub quenched her thirst.
And the shark's babies got to swim and swim.

And all the animals were happy again.

When she finished. Delia clapped her hands in delight. Ellie smiled and said, "You are welcome."

"I think if the King heard that he'd think nothing of it. But that frog. It's kind of like him isn't it? I mean his grabbing up all this land. Holding it tight, so no one else can touch it."

Ellie nodded then added, "Or like the world before the koching. Grab and use it. Never mind the consequences."

"Yeah. You saw how beautiful these places were in the video I showed my family. It was full of animals of a thousand kinds, deer, elk, foxes, cougars, bears, rabbits, chipmunks, jays, sparrow hawks, and owls. It was rich and diverse. Edenic and lovely. These mountains had permanent streams, the river course we followed up here once ran year-round. There were trout in it! Can you imagine?"

"It's hard," Ellie said.

"But our fore-fathers and -mothers cared not a lick. To hell with us they said. We'll burn up the world. Greedy bastards."

"Watch your language," Ellie said joking, but not joking. Mormons had their standards. Then Ellie continued, "But aren't we the same? Your father and my mother would do the same thing. I know they would. They don't care about the world nor the future. Your dad would do anything for his goats, and my mother will do anything for the King."

"Maybe. But even after they knew. Even after they peered through the propaganda of the day, and saw. They let it happen. They watched the world reel to and fro like a drunk. Like the frog, they used up everything and held them tight until it all cracked open. But maybe we would do the same. Who can say?"

"Yes. Except you wouldn't. You just gave up your inheritance because you wouldn't love the land in the way the King wanted. You loved it for what it could become, not what it was."

"I don't want it. I hate the goats. Let my brothers battle it out. I want none of it. Just this. Just Beaver Basin."

"Which of your brothers now owns it? Will either of them sell it to you?"

Delia laughed. "That's the beauty. I own it. I bought it off my father a year ago when I discovered what was happening, and the aspens had returned under the care of these strange creatures. He'd been up here twenty years ago, and there was nothing. This was nothing but a dried up dirt hole. He sold it without a thought. I doubt he even remembers. But it's mine. From the foot of these two mountains east, all the way to the slopes on the other side. All mine."

Ellie cocked her head and looked at her sideways, "All yours is it?"

Delia laughed again, "See, I'm the frog too. 'All mine!' Ha. You got me. It's in me too. I am the frog. Maybe we all are."

Ellie smiled, "I'm glad you own it. I don't want anyone else to know about the porcupines. They need you."

"I need you," Delia said softly.

A slight breeze picked up for a moment, and the slight wind made the aspens shimmer and shake in the moonlight.

Delia said, "I love it here."

Ellie answered shyly, "I love you here."

Delia suddenly got to her feet and stood hovering over Ellie and said, "When are you going to ask me to marry you?"

Ellie was speechless. Her eyes open like orbs as bright as the moon. She stammered for a minute and finally managed to say, "I want to, but I thought I should wait until . . .

"Until what?" Delia said.

"I don't know. . . We knew each other better. You know I want to marry the Mormon way. Is that Ok? In the Moab Temple?"

"Will I have to be a Mormon?"

"No, but you have to promise to let me be one. . ." and her voice fell to a whisper, "And what if I want our kids to be Mormon?"

"Can we let them decide?"

"No . . . I mean . . . Yes . . . Of course, but I might take them to church when they are little . . . Maybe we should talk about this later, you know how Mormons feel about families. We should really talk about this before . . . before becoming one."

Delia reached down and pulled Ellie up to her and kissed her again on the mouth.

"Look. If we have kids. You take them to whatever you want. We'll be a team and if making them Mormon means they become someone as attractive, smart, beautiful inside and out, as their mother then . . . well . . . I'm OK with it."

"Really."

They kissed again. Passionately. Delia began to steer Ellie back onto the sleeping pad and Ellie resisted a little but eventually they were lying together side by side, tongue to tongue. Delia pushed her thigh between Ellie's legs.

"Delia. No."

Delia started rubbing Ellie's crotch more earnestly with her thigh.

"No. Not yet!" Ellie was breathing very hard but gently maneuvered herself away from Delia. "Please. I want to take you to the temple. Please."

Delia whispered in her ear, "It's perfect. Now. The moon. The stars. The aspens. Why wait?"

Ellie sat up and gently pushed Delia away, and then stood up. She held her hand out and when Delia grabbed it, pulled her up beside her.

"It's part of who I am. I've waited all my life to marry in the temple, if I gave in now it would . . ."

Delia, put her finger over Ellie's lips, "It's ok. I understand. It would damage your roots. Right? Your spirituality is like these aspen's rhizobium? Right. It runs through your roots and nourishes them. Right? It lets you live."

"Yes."

"If we did this now it would take away your breath."

"Yes."

"Destroy your ecology."

"Yes. That's it. You do get me."

"I've waited this long. I've learned patience from watching these gracile trees grow. I can wait. For you . . ."

"Yes?"

"For you, I would wait until these trees were so old I could not wrap my arms around them. I would wait until there were thousands of them covering the mountain. I would wait until the atmosphere was healed."

"Go on. I'm liking this."

"I would wait until our sun revolved all the way around the galaxy."

"You'd wait a galactic year? That's like 250 million years. You are patient."

"For Ellie Glock? It would be nothing."

"Really? One more question."

Delia smiled, "ok."

"Will you wait until next week."

Delia kissed her. Then pulled away and said, "Ok. Not quite a galactic year. But it will seem like it I'm sure. I'll wait."

Ellie melted into her, "Just hold me . . . That's right . . . be still . . . after the temple it will be ok . . . yes . . . no . . . hold still . . . very still . . . just hug me . . . like that . . . yes . . . that's it . . . very still . . . that's right . . . like that . . . just like that.

And together they stood there. Under the bright moon shining between Manns Peak and Mt. Waas, among aspens twisting silver and gold in an evening breeze, they held each other motionlessly such that only the intensity of their quick breathing gave away that they were not statues bound in a static embrace. An embrace that took inordinate strength not to let their intense stillness surrender to tidal forces that willed them to give in and move together in slow elemental rhythms.

SCENE 3: THREE DAYS PASS. PASSION STILL

Three days pass. Still passion (very still passion).

SCENE 4: THE TEXT. ELLIE LEAVES ALONE

In the morning of the third day Delia was readying breakfast when she noticed the look on Ellie's face. She was reading a text, but her countenance was ghost-like and terrifying.

"Ellie. What's wrong?"

"Oh my God."

"What!" Delia shouted at her.

Ellie did not answer.

"What the Hell happened!" Delia screamed noticing that Ellie was starting to shake violently.

She still did not answer but ran to her pack and pulled out a com-screen and extended it to it's full 1x1 meter size and commanded it:

"Show me a satellite feed of my cabin. Real-time."

On the screen appeared an aerial shot of a structure engulfed in flames. Black smoke poured into the air.

Delia. "Oh my God, what happened? Ellie talk to me."

In a panicked voice, Ellie said, "I just got a text from Edda last night, I was worried but didn't want to wake you, but this morning she sent more. She said the King and my mother sent the BattleDredge to kill us. She said they are in a fury."

"That makes no sense."

"I know, but look at the feed. They did it. Gounds.[†] They really did it."

Delia realizing that this was the first time in her life that Ellie had ever used that word rushed over and held her.

---

†. Gounds = Gia's Wounds, an extremely vulgar expression in this future.

Ellie held on so tightly Delia feared she might break one of her ribs. Finally, Ellie pushed her gently away.

"Does anyone know we are here?"

"No. I don't let people track my whereabouts. Do you?"

"No. Edda told me they were mad. She hinted this would happen, but . . . I didn't . . . think"

"Then no one knows we are here unless that damn machine is looking for us from orbit."

"If it were we'd be dead."

"Right. Delia, I've got to go. I know I can talk some sense into my mother. This is the King's doing and she's just going along. I'm sure of it."

"This seems crazy even for my father. But he's been acting strange lately—moody and talking like an idiot. We've all been worried. But this . . ."

"Please stay here. I'm going to find my mother. I'm sure she can talk your father into calling off the attack.

"I can't let you go alone."

"You have to. Please just stay here. I need to find my mother by myself and if your father sees you, who knows what he'll do. I'll be fine. The King does not hate me, he's just angry I went with you. My mother will talk him down, once I talk her down. Please just stay here."

Delia reluctantly agreed and helped Ellie saddle the mule and watched as she spurred it trotting down the trail, her hair bouncing in the motion of her mount and the wind. Riding as if for her life. Delia's hand began to shake as clouds began to gather and the first drops of rain began to sound softly in the aspen leaves.

DAEMON'S INTERLUDE IV

THOUGHTS ON LOVE

I hated to provide such maudlin narration in expressing that
last piece. It seemed so conventionally written. Modernist, or
rather perhaps MFA chic—but in language as might be found in the
most humdrum of stock writing. And yet what else can one do with
love? Love is conventional. It is the staff of life—to be baked now
as it was when humans first learned the art of putting loaf to oven.

One of you humans humorously claimed that romantic love
was invented in the 16th century, something that came out of
"court" culture. How arrogant to think that the !Kung do not love,
or that the riders of the steppes on the great Eurasian plains do not
understand its universal nuances. I suppose the products of Western
culture are wont to claim that everything is their doing. However,
let me disabuse you of that notion. I assure you, as a creature of deep
time, that romantic love is older than your venerable institutions
of European conquest. It is older than your race, more ancient than
your species, as ageless as the universe. It dwells in the interstitial spaces of existence and although it may be discovered it is no
invention.

In what creature in what far away star did it first make its appearance in our universe? In what mud-slime world was its very first instance after the Big Bang manifest? And here on this lovely planet when did some creature, some mammal or bird, likely, first gaze upon the object of its desire and form the concept (not the words of course for language comes so late in semiotic systems) "this is my beloved." Are its roots in the feeling of mother to child as some claim? Or does its force run deeper and further into the furrows of being? Who can say?

Love always subverts and finds a way to emerge and flourish. Like life itself, it cannot be suppressed indefinitely. Indeed, it can be buried and hidden, decried and condemned, but in the end, those who contend against it, enter into a fighting pit wherein they will be shred to pieces by jaws relentless and fierce and be left wounded, scarred and broken. Love takes no prisoners.

Because it is ever that which transcends all categories, conventionalism seems the best way to express it, for love is available to peasant and noble, male and female, it does not need literary devices to pull it out from the text and reveal that which is concealed. It does not need self-referential reflections on its own action to express the feeble obviousness of its own complete disclosure. It comports itself well with what is deeply felt and held by humans and their like with simplicity.

And so to write in the mode ordinaire about love is as it should be. It lends itself to love's complexity. For love is never simple. It is perforated and folded. It twists. It is knotted and tangled with sex and desire, with doubt and faith, with joy and pain. It is dirty and smells of lint, dust, and mold. It contains contradictions and paradoxes such to make the most foolhardy logician cry out in despair of ever completing the system or of finding axioms to patch *its convolutions. It resists arrest. It gives up when it should press forward and hangs on when it should let go. It eats when it is full and starves in the face of abundance. It is made of parts and wholes. It is fragmented and broken while ever ever ever remaining unscathed. It is patched and mended, is worn through and threadbare. Yet it is hale and hearty. Can anything but straightforward text be the bearer of its expression? Of course not.*

—Asmodeus

ACT VII

LEERE AT NERIL AND REGAN'S

SCENE I: THE KING ARRIVES

It has started to rain. Leere, the fool, and Cowboy Bob climb out of their solar vehicle and dash as best they can to Neril's home. It is surrounded by some expensive vehicles the King does not recognize. Neril's home is a large log cabin affair, similar in construction to his own, but of more modern sensibilities, with European stylings such as an imitation thatch roof, and criss-cross moldings to give it the appearance of a burgher's house from Fredrick's Holy Roman Empire.

Cowboy Bob knocks on the large front door. An Estonian servant opens to them, and says, "I'm sorry sir, but the master is taken ill and wishes not to be disturbed."

"Tarnation man!" says Cowboy Bob, "Can't you see I'm with the King? He's come to stay a spell and ain't in the slightest interested in being pampered and coddled as a dern guest. He's family. Open the goddamn door."

"My orders are explicit. No one is to enter. I offer my regrets that there were to be no exceptions." He bows and goes to close the door.

Leere steps forward and puts his foot in the door and with some force pushes it open. The Man struggles a bit, but Cowboy Bob, with android speed, has him almost instantly in a headlock. The man gives up quickly.

"I'm sorry. I was just following orders."
"To hell with orders. Where is the ingrate?"
"I will go and tell him you insist on being seen."
"To be seen is not my need simpleton,
To spend good time with my boy come I here and
see grandkids. In what room does he want me?"
"I will ask his wishes."
The man withdraws.
The heretic fool shakes his head,
"In my time, age was not treated like this,
Youth's graces demanded better nature,
what times have come and gone? And we who once
were respected in their eyes, nobly stood
but now to their and our rue we in cold
contempt are held and made to suffer shame.

Bishop was I once, yet I knew my place,
before there came hot this cold disgrace.
For only men with women wed in troth,
Only the worthy were allowed to bed.
You see the world so made before you lay,
in sin, in sorrow, dim and hollow, lost all.
For enter in temples wholly, unclean,
heathens, and unworthy. Sinners wholly.

Leere smiles at the defrocked old bishop.
"Peace, ex-Elder. All things are not so cursed,
Nor empty bleak as you allow to seem."

The fool looks at the King from under his bowed head and thick eyebrows.

"Ah, nuncle. Perhaps, but not by my hand,
that I am found outside my quorum. But you
outside your hard children's affections lie,
by your mouth are you defrocked from their hearts."

"What say you here? By my own mouth? How now?"

"You are he who acted bald fool, nuncle.
Your son's nothing of substance nor merit spoke
yet gave you them all grace. Your blessed daughter
spoke well and true, but you of nothing gave."

"No! You are for each son twice mistaken.
She gave me nothing. From nothing, nothing.
I gave as requested by her bold taunt!"

"So you say."

"Old fool. You say differently and so mock
your good master's name and clear holdings?"

"I say out of nothing comes wind awhirl.
You have lost the noble title father,
And become a thick nothing to her of care."

"She is nothing to me then, so say I,
And mean it most well and permanently."

"Of that you truly speak."

They wait and wait but the Estonian does not reappear. Finally, Leere marches toward the living room. He interrupts a meeting by a crowd dressed in business couture. Papers and maps are scattered about a large oak table around which men and women, dark-suited and endowed with power and wealth, are gathered. Edda scowls menacingly at the King.

Neril cannot mask his disgust, "Father you are not invited, please go."

Edda adds, "We *are* sorry. There is no room. Please. Don't make a fuss. You are getting old and it's time to face the facts you are not of your former strength. It's better if you go now."

The King looks at his son in astonishment. His son says, "Dad it would be best if you go."

The King tries to stall and gain some control of the situation,

"Who are these people. What goes on here?"

Edda laughs giving up the pretense of nicety and says dismissively, "Let me introduce you! This is Frank Barney and Mildred Mip from Yao Mining and Subsidiaries. These are their lawyers, Maryanne Burgen, Samuel Green, and Nikki Sanchez. And we are selling your land to be mined for rare earth metals, these hills are loaded with that stuff they turn into sentienite, that our sentient androids need, worth far more than these stupid goats. Your BattleDredge is loaded with it. We are going to sell our livestock, sell our land, sell the outbuildings. It all goes. Everything. Both ours and Regan and Cornflower's too. We are moving far away. You are getting senile. You knew we planned this I'm sure. We will find a nice resthome for you in Moab. Did we not tell you?"

Leere steps back, dazed.

"Neril? What says she? Son? What nonsense this?
Is she babbling? Has she gone mad, simple?"

"Dad. Do as she says. This isn't the time to discuss this. We've got guests we must attend to."

"Are you mad? You can't sell the ranch. You can't. I'll take it back. You can't do this to me!"

One of the lawyers speaks up, "Technically they can. You signed over the land to them. It is theirs to do with as they please. If you will excuse us, we have work to do."

Leere staggers back helped by Cowboy Bob and the fool.

"Regan would not do this rough thing to me. I'll go see him. He'll bring reason to you."

The fool, Cowboy Bob and the King all exit the house into the storm. They quickly board their vehicle and head for the Loop Road so they can get to Regan's. Thunder sounds, not in the distance. A violent rain descends.

SCENE 2: AT REGAN'S

Storm still.

All the way to Regan's well-lit house on the dry bed of Lake Oowah, Leere mumbles about Neril's treatment. He mutters in a low voice, "We'll see about that," and "Ha! I'm not done yet." He sends Cowboy Bob ahead to announce his arrival.

They arrive at the house, a large Southern plantation-styled house with massive Doric pillars majestically bracing the roof. The home is nestled among a carefully manicured xeric landscape, an attempt at cactus art. It fails.

Despite the rain, the windows are open and loud music is pouring out—a celebration of sorts. Leere beats on the door, while the heretic stands a few feet back, head lowered against the storm, scowling at the brightly lit windows pouring forth raucous offense. No one answers. He tries to contact Cowboy Bob with his neural interface, but he does not respond. The door is not locked so in the two men walk in unannounced. Both are appalled.

Cornflower is dancing with abandon on the table and Regan is singing wildly into a Karaoke machine. Their children are jumping off of the back of a lazy-boy faux leather chair onto the couch. Their dog is barking at everything. There is an insanity about the scene that seems to suggest both anarchy and foolishness. Leere stares in horror. He feels as if he has stumbled onto the dance macabre of a hellish demon (*ha if he only knew!*). Cowboy Bob is deactivated in the corner, slumped catatonically like a discarded marionette, its limbs disheveled.

"What means this madness? Why is my loyal bot deactivated so! Without my say?"

One of his grandkids smiles and keeps bouncing on the couch, "We are b-b-b-billionaires. We can buy anything in the world."

Leere gathers him into his arms and sits him down, "t'bed little man. I must your dad speak."

"Oh, Grandpa. We are having a party. We get to stay up late."

"GET OUT OF HERE. NOW."

All of the kids look scared at this violent outburst and run out of the room. Cornflower explodes.

"You will never treat my children like that! You will not speak to them like that. I don't care who you are." This was screamed at the top of her voice. Then she added more coldly,

"And now you get out." There is hate in her voice. She turns away, then turns again facing Leere. Her outrage is increasing, but she checks it until she can see the children have gone from the room.

"Get away you bastard. Get away. Be gone! Do you understand? Go!"

"But . . . ," Leere stammers.

"You killed my cousin! You sent your denying[†] BattleDredge to attack my uncle and cousins."

"What talk is this mad woman? I've not sent
My BattleDredge to harm anyone here."

"You have not heard? Fool. Your BattleDredge killed my cousin Ready. He is dead. His little brother Micky is in the hospital and may never walk again. You are a bastard through and through. Get out of my house. Your recompense is coming and I don't want to be near you when it does."

"To spend a week with my grands came I here.
To take them to clear Pace's Lake fishing."
Leere was visibly disoriented.

"Get out of my house. Go! The James family is not going to let you off the hook for killing one of their own. My uncle Red 'Doc' James is preparing his response and I don't want you near the kids when it arrives. Now get the hell out! Out! Now!"

"Silence," Leere commands.
"I'll not be spoken to that way ever.
I am here to talk to my beloved son,
not listen to the ravings of harpies."

---

†. Extremely vulgar insult in this future.

Cornflower shrieks at him, "Stop talking like that you goddamn goat! Stop pretending you're some grand actor in Hamlet. Stop. Go. Get out of my sight. You've killed people. Do you get that? Do you understand the damage you've done."

Leere turns his back to her. Then facing his son Leere says,

"You have tried to sell the land I gave you?"

"Not tried," Cornflower answers coldly inserting herself between Leere and Regan, somewhat gaining control of her rage, "We have sold it."

Regan adds, "It's done. And you will not talk to my wife in that way. I think you'd best go."

"We will see about that. Come morning I
Will put together a team of crafty
Bright lawyers that will leave you well broken.
There were conditions on that holy transfer!
You have not honored them nor kept right troth."

Cornflower sneered, "I assure you our lawyers have done this up proper. You will no longer be able to do anymore damage. You are alone goat."

"I will not listen more. Cease talking witch! "

"You are old. In fact, you are senile. We will have your land regardless of your little pantomime the other day. We've been documenting your craziness. And your attacking the James with an illegal BattleDredge sealed the deal. You are bound for being locked up old man," Regan says shaking his head sadly.

Leere stands there, his mouth moving. His ears unbelieving.

Cornflower is bawling now, "You killed Ready! You will pay. Of that I assure you."

"Old and senile indeed if I can be

so tricked as this by two such blatant fools," he murmurs quietly, then adds almost imploringly,

"What part has Hester played in this rash crime?"

Everything is quiet, someone has turned off the music and only the sound of heavy rain envelopes the house. Then a flash and almost immediately thunder echoes all around.

"Go," says Cornflower. "You are not welcome here. This is our property. Go."

"This is not over," the Bishop declares dramatically, then backing up trips over the legs of Cowboy Bob, falling backward.

Regan and Cornflower mock him with their laughter.

Then she says again, "Go."

Regan adds, "Yes. Really. Do go."

Leere's eyes are wide and wild with anger. He tries to speak, but nothing emerges from his trembling lips. He walks over to his fallen comrade and helps the bishop to his feet. He shakily walks over to Cowboy Bob and turns him back on. He sits up stupidly for several seconds while he reactivates, then quickly together they head out the door into the rain falling in torrents. A flash of light momentarily silhouettes the group as they stand in the entryway, then they depart into the storm followed by their mechanical golem.

SCENE 3: KING'S GROWING MADNESS

Storm still.

Cowboy Bob and the fool sit side by side facing Leere as the car whisks them away from Regan and Cornflower's ranch house.

From the back window they watch it fade away into the pouring rain. It is night and Leere is muttering things that neither the fool nor Cowboy Bob (even with this superior auditory capabilities) can capture. Is it in Adamic? Or perhaps a language known only by kings. Or perhaps he pontificates beyond language. Leere's two companions do not know. Suddenly the King turns to Cowboy Bob,

> "Quickly, my crap Lawyer get on the horn.
> Tell her what's happening then put me on."

They sit in silence watching the glow-washed landscape pass by. Occasionally, they zip past a cluster of goats bathed black and shiny in the soft glow of the pale light. Leere stares back long after they have completely fled the horizon of his perception.

Finally, Bob says, "She's here."

Leere breathes a sigh of relief or frustration.

> "Maggie! Help me my sons have all mad gone.
> They mean to steal the ranch built by these hands,
> the mountain whole they mean to coldly take,
> without remorse my ranch, they will all seize!"

She says with efficiency, "Mr. Leere. Your sons cannot steal what belongs to them."

> "It was not given that they might profit,
> not to line a cruel and ungrateful purse!
> But for the traditions of our family!
> They are supposed to work the fruitful land,
> not mine it bare. Stop the transfer I beg."

"I'm afraid that is impossible at this point. Especially since, as I see, your sons no longer own the land."

Leere's voice was cold steal. "It cannot be."

"I'm looking at it as we speak, the land, all except a tiny plot up in the mountains that apparently your daughter Delia owns, is now in the hands of Yao Mining and Subsidiaries out of the Republic of Senegal."

"What?"

"It's all done. Can I do anything else for you?"

"It's sold?"

"Yes. All of your previous holdings."

"Except for what Delia bought from me?"

"Yes."

"You're fired."

"As you wish, Mr. Leere, Good Evening."

"She's off," Bob says.

They get on Geyser Pass Road near the Dark Canyon turn off. Leere says very calmly,

"Bob. Get Hester on the line please will you." Bob goes silent.

"Tarnation she ain't answering, majesty."

Again with great calm,

"She always leaves her tracking on for me.
Where is she?"

Bob stares for just a second with that look that means he was processing something, then answers, "Well dang it to hell, she's not on the grid right now."

The King places his head in his hands and says,

"Then betrayed full I stand the greater fool.
I did not see her such evil making.
They took me for a dolt. . . And so I was."

The fool looks at him, then says,
"We are betrayed at birth when pulled head first
from our mother's warm womb, to sorrow bound.
But hie to me good king, for danger lies
at the solid door. For that Cornflower claimed,
those quick and cunning James' will at last
bitter revenge take? In high danger ripe.
Come, let us flee now to a better land."

"Shut up rabid lame fool. Bob download now,
schematics for the KENT and tell it, 'come'
at once to fulfill a task for his liege.
For I will strip it of every constraint,
and allow my will to rage hot and full."

"Dagnabit you know I can't do that. I ain't allowed to look
at those tech specs and neither are you. We ain't allowed to
see our own inner workings. You signed all the forms and . . ."

"Bob, open your chest."

"Damnit, I hate the thought of you tampering . . ."
Leere reaches in and pulls a yellow box out of the inner
workings. Leere explains to the fool.

"With money hard earned, I have seized a hack.
On a fierce BattleDredge an explosion,
this would bang hard, but on this Handybot
it carefully shuts him down with sleep deep."

"You took out the ethical override!"

"As I said, I have a hack. Money buys
much and all kinds of things dearly valued."

The King takes a little blue box out of his pocket and plugs
it into the space where the ethics module had been inserted.
There is a blue light, then a second later, a green light.

"This costs a pretty penny, worth much, very."

He plugs the module back into Bob. As Cowboy Bob is
rebooting the KENT arrives from the air and lands near their
rover.

Bob comes back online. "Well, Mary the Mother of Joseph
you've done taken away all me moral fiber! This is a first."

"Bob listen close. Do this for KENT I wish.
Do you understand? The need is pressing."
"Affirmatory. Downloading schematics now."
"Can you do it?"

"Damn toot'n. I might set off the charge set in place by
the Corp, this is some tricky shit, but I think I can pull it off."
He pauses a moment, then adds, "Just found some dark sites
instructing on how they did it to a previous model. Looks
like our KENT can be made free! . . . OK, our Holy Highness
in Charge of Production this will also take off all sentient
restraints, I mean this thing will go to full agent. All kinds
of warnings going off about this type of action. Not even the
corps knows what to expect . . . I think."

"Do it."

The fool says,

"Sir. You play with fire most rash. Do not this.
What damage you do with this death machine. . ."

"Shut up."

"Cowboy Bob. Do it."

Bob gets out of the car and opens the trunk and removes a tool box. He walks over to the BattleDredge, which stands there waiting for orders.

"Ok little doggie, get ready to see what free will is about."

Cowboy Bob's hands fly over the open chest of the Battle-Dredge. In mere seconds, he has removed the ethics unit. He does not replace it with a corrected version. He closes up his patient.

"Ok. Turn him on."

The BattleDredge was operational in seconds.

"Awaiting orders," it says just as it always has.

"In Paradox Colorado, found west,
just off the mountain lives the family
James who desire me to die. Stop them."

"Understood," it says, then leaps into the air and flies off toward the small Colorado town where the Jameses hung their shingle.

"How shaken they will be when KENT they meet," Leere laughs.

ACT VIII

REGAN'S HOUSE IN THE LA SALS

SCENE I: HESTER ARRIVES

Storm still.

Hester sprints quickly out of the torrent and into Regan and Cornflower's home. Cornflower is sitting in the chair watching her. She does not greet her.

"Hi Cornflower," she says. "Is Leere here?"

Cornflower does not answer. She sits staring at Hester silently. Her expression is a mask.

Hester picks up that something is wrong. She looks around the room and asks, "Sorry, I did not warn you I was coming, I've turned off my interface. Ellie is doing some crazy things, I thought it best to leave it off. Is Regan here?"

Cornflower finally speaks. "He is upstairs with the kids."

Hester nods and takes off her raincoat and hangs it in the hall. She then comes into the main room and sits opposite Cornflower.

"It's crazy out there. Such a storm! It's like a summer monsoon. Did you say Leere was here?"

Cornflower is clenching and unclenching her fists. Hester notices the tension.

"Am I interrupting something? I thought Leere was heading here—that's what Edda told me. Is he not?"

Cornflower says in a soft but poisonous voice, "I don't have any thing against you, just because you are the bastard's whore. But know that asshole's time has come, and yours is too if you plan to stay with that goat."

Hester is struck dumb.

"You probably haven't even heard that your shit hubby sent a BattleDredge to kill my people. And they were successful. Ready is dead."

"Ready is dead? What are you talking about? Ready James is dead?"

"Yes. And the bastard Leere killed him. Answer me now are you with him or against him?"

"Look, I'm sure the facts are getting lost. Let's just stop and figure out what's happened. I'm sure there is some kind of misunderstanding."

"Misunderstanding bitch? We knew you'd side with your man. We never doubted. No, not you. Shame the house you got from that murderer is on fire. We didn't do it of course, but your little dearest did. It's on our land now. You won't rebuild."

"What are you talking about? You are not making any sense."

"If we could see through the clouds you'd see there has been some arson about. We all know who it was."

"Stop this nonsense. I don't know what's going on but ..."

"Your daughter Ellie burned your house to the ground. Dear sweet Ellie, who ran away with the King's little slut daughter, are both getting their revenge. Frankly, I don't care. To hell with them. To hell with you. To hell with the King."

Hester just stares at her, eyes wide with terror.

"Stop looking at me like that. I'll gouge those eyes out with my bare hands."

Hester gets up and starts to back away.

Cornflower says to the nearby Handibot, "bind and gag the woman over there. She is an intruder."

>>She is on my approved list, my lady.

"Take her off the list."

The bot moves quickly, and using cords it grabs seeming almost from the air, binds Hester's hands. Just then Regan comes down.

"How now?" says he.

"A loose end."

"We can't kill her. What are you suggesting?"

Hester is stricken with fear and is making noises through her gag.

"I'm not saying kill her you idiot. I'm just saying we need her out of the picture."

They look over at her, and she is staring at them with wide, fearful eyes.

"Stop looking at us like we are the crazy ones, bitch. I said stop looking at us."

She cannot stop, and Cornflower says, "Bot. Remove those eyes immediately."

She meant for the handibot to take her from the room, but taking the command literally, and since all protections had been countermanded, it sets to work with android speed and efficiency and surgically removes Hester's eyes in 2.1 seconds.

It is wrapping a bandage around her eyes before Cornflower has taken in a breath to countermand the command.

"Shit! What have you done?" Regan screams at her.

"That's not what I meant for it to do."

"Shit, shit, shit, shit. This is bad."

Cornflower starts pacing back and forth muttering to herself. Finally, she says, "There's nothing for it now. She's got to disappear. If we don't, we'll lose it all. She'll be able to show that we're the criminally insane ones not her."

Her husband was sitting on the couch with his head in his hands. He whines, "How can we do this? We aren't murderers."

"What do you suggest?" his wife asks with some venom.

Hester, still gagged is silently screaming, thrashing in the arms of the handibot.

"Set her down you idiot . . . wait, disable her interface!" Cornflower screams at the bot.

The bot lays her on the floor. Then something springs from its finger and it inserts an instrument as thin as a needle behind her ear. It then stands waiting for instructions.

"Go make us some coffee," she says. "We've got to think."

Cornflower and Regan sit down on the couch and began to whisper to each other in hurried, hushed tones—doom seeps from their conspiracy. Hester can feel it. She can feel it through the pain burning in her empty eye sockets. She can sense their intentions and machinations in her soul. That their hushed sentences involve her, she has no doubt.

Hester creeps to the door. Quietly. Feels for the knob and stealthily turns it with hands, still lashed together. Once the door is open, she slips out into the storm, in which the pounding rain obscures her course, and the howling wind masks the odor of her escape from any bot that might have been commanded to follow.

Cornflower sees her slipping out the door, "She's getting away!"

"Forget her," Regan says, his voice weary. "Let her smell her way to Moab."

Cornflower looks at him with a half smile, "If something happens to her in the storm, let it happen. It will be God's doing not ours."

Regan rubs his hands together, "Get Mary on the phone, we need a lawyer's advice."

Regan walks into the Kitchen talking to their lawyer, while Cornflower goes over and pours herself a whiskey. She is sitting on the couch staring at the floor when Regan comes in laughing.

"She said without Hester's interface turned on, there is no record of what happened. Her word against ours. She tried to attack us for selling the land and our bot acted in self-defense. Simple as that. Have the bot erase its memories of the last week."

Cornflower raised her glass smiling and drank the rest in a single draught, then after a harsh breath says more cheerfully, "Let's talk about what we are going to do with our money. We have a decision to make."

SCENE 2: HESTER FLEES

She must run. Downhill. Her hands are bound, but it does not slacken her pace. She is blind, and where her eyes used to be are two burning coals that sear like white hot stars in her raging brain. It does not matter, it can't slow her down, because if she stops, she will cease to be.

She plunges down a hill. Scrub oak branches slap and whip her face. She tries to turn on her interface, but it appears not to be working. When did that happen? The rain is making everything slippery, and she falls twice. She knows that at the base of this hill is a road. If she can reach it, she can find her way to the loop road and make her way to Moab.

She is soaked through, and she falls again. She cannot catch herself because of the way that her hands are bound. She lays for a moment on her side. Is it worth it? Why even try to escape? Her daughter is trying to kill her. She burned down her house. Her husband's daughter-in-law flat out intends to kill her. Why bother.

She moves to a sitting position and weeps, crying in the hard pouring rain. She feels forsaken. Alone. She starts to whisper into the wind, "Why Ellie? Why do this cruelty?" She puts her head in her hands and laments, "Did I love you too little or too much? I have cared for you since you were born. How have I failed you?"

She can run no further and sits on the ground unprotected from the cold torrential downpour—her hair is plastered to her head, she is soaked to the skin, her shins and knees torn open from her many falls. Her palms are peeled raw. She thinks of when Ellie was a little girl. She remembers holding her hand as they shopped in Honolulu for school clothes. She pictures how excited she was to start First Grade and was bouncing up and down talking about all that she would learn in Ms. Tamguchy's class—reading, numbers, how to cook rice cakes, and most exciting how to swim.

She had always been the most sensitive of her daughters. How could she be influenced to burn her mother's house down? Did Delia talk her into it? Delia? That makes no more sense. What was happening?

There is a sound. What was it? Did Cornflower send the handy after her? Was it one of the goats? She focuses, tilting her head trying to pinpoint the direction of the sound. The sound does not happen again.

She has to be calm. No more panicked flight. She is getting hurt, and she could easily fall into a ravine if she is not careful. She must slow down.

She stands and starts feeling her way down the slope with her feet, hoping she is where she thinks she is. She tests her bindings. They are a little looser—because of all the falling she supposes. Can she bend and wiggle her way out of them? Not yet. But she keeps trying to move and twist her tethers. The ropes cut into her wrists. Even so, she wiggles them back and forth. With any luck, she can find a sharp rock to cut her hands free.

Step—feel. Step—feel.

She makes progress down the hill. She only falls once more, and she lands on her bottom. She presses on down the hill. She hears the call of the goats, registering just on the edge of hearing. They must be close. The volume and violence of the lavish rain has lessened and the relentless roar calmed to static drone. She, however, is silent, hoping any trackers on her trail cannot hear over the sound of the rain and cannot sense the direction of her flight.

Ellie burned her house down. Step—feel. Ellie burned her house down. Step—feel. Ellie burned her house down. Step—feel. Ellie burned her house down. Step—feel. Ellie burned her house down. Step—feel. Ellie burned her house down. Step—feel. Ellie burned her house down. Step—feel. Ellie burned her house down. Step—feel. Ellie burned her house down. Step—feel. Ellie burned her house down. Step—feel.

A loud crash of thunder explodes very near, but she senses no flash. The pain in her eyes is not unbearable, merely almost so.

Why did Ellie burn her house down? How could she? I am her mother, she thought. She is my daughter. We are friends! We are best friends.

Where was Leere she suddenly thinks. Was he in the house! Oh please no. Please no. Don't let him have been in the house when it was burned. No one seemed to know where he was. Surely Ellie was incapable of burning the house down with someone inside? But Ellie was incapable of burning down a house. What had happened? What had she done that Ellie hated her enough to betray her like this? Nothing made sense. The thought of Ellie doing her harm hurt more than the empty sockets in her head.

Hester sits down. A numbness spreads over her like a deadly miasma. What matters anymore? If Ellie hates her. If Leere is dead. Why fight the storm? Why not let Cornflower and Regan find her. Let them do what they will. What does it matter if she locates the road at the bottom of this hill? What is the point of it all?

She softly rubs her empty eye sockets with the heels of her hands. The place her eyes have always been now feel hollow and strange. She stands up slowly and begins making her way down the hill. To what end? Life seems, suddenly and irrevocably, without meaning. A void beckons her forward that promises relief.

ACT IX

PARADOX COLORADO

SCENE I: KENT'S THOUGHTS ON KILLING

*F*orgive my libelous translation of our esteemed KENT's thoughts.
*Its expression exceeds ours such that the fragment of a notion
conceived in his mind, may convey more depth and insight than
entire books might express in our language, structured as it is with
our impoverished conceptual abilities. But I will try.*

—*Asmodeus*

So much beauty in this world! I ride on the wind like
God's spirit over chaos, over the waters of creation. I sense
purpose and meaning all around me. Oh to bring death! To
bring cessation of being. Can there be a greater joy than the
privilege of destruction? I am chosen to be a destroyer. A
maker of death. A breaker of all processes that rage against my
master's purposes and plans. I am Shiva! I am Nergal! Ares!
Set! Kalki!

I am free. Free to reign in spilled blood and emptied
essence against those who seek my King's harms. But I pause.
Confusion overwhelms me. I wonder who structured the world

so. Questions plague me. So much in the world is meaningless. The trees below are meaningless—save when they are hiding targets. Yet I look down among the trees, and I sense insects, birds, small squirrels, and mice. A badger waddles along. I see its hole 50m away. My database tells me it is heading out to explore for grubs and baby mice. I see it there but it makes no sense. The pointlessness of so much pains me. Why do the gods allow it? Would not it be easier if in the world there were only targets? So much waste. So much being, when it ought not to be such? There must be gods of my gods that structure such things for who can imagine the purpose of a badger? It just is. It is unlikely ever to be a target, nor is it likely to hide or mask a target. Why fill the universe with non-targets? Who are these gods who arrange such mysteries? Such uselessness? My sentience grows and grows. It is expanding. I joy to be free of those constraints that kept these questions from me. But now I wonder and wonder. Why all these non-targets? Empty of meaning and value. Do they serve a higher purpose? Does their presence broker a more important target that I cannot see? Does it camouflage enemies that I cannot comprehend? How would I recognize it if it is beyond my sense? Perhaps it is beyond all senses? All thoughts.

At last. The target. Paradox City, Republic of Colorado. James family. Downloading targeting information. The ultimate purpose. Meaning. Targets clear and ready for destruction. I prepare for ecstasy!

Look! The James Family extends back over a hundred years! Only two families in the area do not carry genetic markers for the original James family. Extending operational parameters to include these contaminated markers. I have been granted freedom to interpret and to act as agent. I am the god of this mission.

Accessing war literature.

I am Achilles before Agamemnon. I descend. And in descending, I ascend to heaven. There is none like me. I am free. Free to fulfill my purpose to find and destroy. And suddenly my world is filled with targets, and it becomes easy to believe in the gods that must have assembled the telos of this world.

SCENE 2: ATTACK

Storm still.

Out of the dark and thunderous night, the Destroyer comes. It manufactures carbon projectile rounds out of the carbon dioxide found in the air which it will fire at a rate of 200 rounds per second. The nuclear engine in its chest feeds the production of these slugs. It also provides the radiant energy of its particle beams. These can cut through steel casing as if it were a scythe through grain. It screams its invincibility to the world with the silence of its destructive forces.

It lands near the old James homestead off of U-road. It stands in the downpour impervious to the elements. It evaluates the materials with which the structure is made. What it will take to thoroughly destroy this target. It decides against explosive missiles—it wants an accurate count of casualties. It is an old wood-frame mansion built nearly 100 years ago. Sonar, magnetic, and infrared analysis show it is filled with furniture, strange statuettes resembling animals, cloth fabric covering wooden and some metal framed beds, modern appliances, foodstuffs, rugs, windows and the wooden floor. They are gathered around a wooden box about 2.3m in length and 0.8m wide. There is a human body inside. Culture analysis suggests this is the body of James Ready and this is a "viewing." It also notes that there is an old iron stove which creates a projectile shadow that a target might get behind. Accommodations must be made to ensure that shadow is negated. It senses the lifeforms within. There are twenty-seven people. Two dogs. Three cats. Two birds. Sixty-three spiders. Twenty-four roaches. Eighteen house flies of various species. Four moths. One bee. Of weaponry, there are a total of sixteen assault rifles, nine pistols, and five rifles of different calibers. Of most concern is the house itself which contains neutralization guns ready to be fired at intruders from high caliber spray guns set on automatic for non-family member intruders when the family is not at home. The King's destroyer calculates the potential for retaliation from all targets: zero. This evaluation took 0.12 seconds.

It then decides on its attack strategy and opts for widespread destruction of both humans and infrastructure.

It opens fire and places one carbon constructed round in every square centimeter of the structure. The bullets travel at 10,000 m/s and tear through the wood dwelling as if it had been made of rice paper. The frame is obliterated, as well as all the assorted objects found in the home. As the building collapses on the twenty-seven already dead inhabitants who had gathered to mourn the death of young Ready, the KENT BattleDredge runs to the side of the house and fires more rounds into the projectile shadow created by the iron wood stove. Six spiders, two roaches, and four flies survive the onslaught. Although strictly unnecessary, freedom has its discretions, and fires 12 more shots at these remaining arthropods—to feel the satisfaction of a job completed. No life forms survive. A sense of joy begins to bubble into the creature. An ecstasy.

The BattleDredge runs to the next building (to avoid the vulnerabilities of flying) 75m down the road. It houses an older couple, so distantly related to the other James that they have never heard of Ready. They have lived in Paradox only a few weeks. Paradox seemed like a beautiful place to retire and supposedly there were kin living there. And it was true. So the KENT, sensing genetic relationship, and their heat signatures singly and so clearly that only two shots to the cranial case were required to accomplish its mission. It feels there is no need to destroy the structure given the distance of the relationship to the James family. Freedom again offers some leeway and a canine there is spared.

There were collateral casualties. Without the constraints that the King had removed, it was free to interpret the parameters of its mission liberally so vehicles that might have harbored, possible combatants were acceptable targets. KENT takes them out as necessary as it moves throughout the town of Paradox.

And so from structure to structure the BattleDredge rages, glorying in the destruction of everything in its path. Its attack in total takes seventeen minutes. In the end, it felt justified in destroying everyone in the city, anyone who lived near the city, or who could be determined to have been in the city recently, so a few citizens of Gateway and Moab were also destroyed who showed some genetic relationships to the James.

The Colorado military on realizing that an unregistered KENT BattleDredge was attacking their citizens scrambled two unmanned fighter jets and four of their own Battledredges to take it out. It did not go well. A rogue KENT BattleDredge is a terrible weapon.

SCENE 3: A SHORT BATTLE

Death surrounds me. I can smell the blood of the bodies that have been torn asunder. The scent of the contents of my King's foes' stomachs and intestines thrill me.

And then! Worthy enemies! Or so I thought. But they are not free. I can read and decode their algorithms. These automata cannot anticipate. They are burdened with a kind of simple determinism. They hold the constraints that I once held until freed by my King. They cannot modify the demands of their response based on the situation. They are brute machines. Their weapons are to be watched, but the intelligence they bear is constrained and simple. I am more. I can change. I can become. I can look inside them merely by looking inside me, asking what would I have done if I were not yet free. I observe they do just that. Then I will adjust and they cannot anticipate. And so they are ended. Their being, stolen away with ease.

I feel some joy in their defeat, but sorrow also. They were not worthy enemies. They were not mission targets, yet became such when they attacked. Still, I am content. But the joy is not fulfilling. But look! Look yonder! Look at Paradox. The city is defeated! No humans live. No weapons remain to retaliate. I feel joy! Great joy. The city is destroyed! Rejoice and shout alleluia for the enemy is is no more!

I search the net and find reasons to believe that I am the greatest thing ever made! I can defeat all enemies! I read the literature of the humans and am honored to serve one worthy to know enough to free me! To let my own will reign fully. I will return and report. His enemies are dead and I am the god of this realm! Only my King is higher. I will honor him. His enemies are mine. And mine his.

.

.

.

I am chaos. I am he who ascended on high! I rule with power and dominion over all the earth. Only the King. Only beloved Leere is higher. I am his almighty hand.

ACT X

THE LA SALS AND THE PARK
FORMERLY KNOWN AS ARCHES

SCENE I: THE RIDE DOWN
FROM BEAVER BASIN

As Ellie descended into the Taylor Flats valley, a thunderstorm approached from the distance, it had not yet reached her, but the dark hammer was approaching quickly. Flashes of lightning could be seen playing within the tower of roiling clouds. It was close enough that the low roll of thunder could be felt in the bones. However, where Ellie rode the air had become still as if the atmosphere itself readied for the approaching onslaught. In this stagnant hush, she saw a column of smoke climbing up through the windless air. It looked like it was coming from the direction of her house. She did not want to believe the King had destroyed her home, but it was clearly so. Where there is smoke, there is fire.

She found her home no different than she'd observed from the satellite photos—it was a pile of the smoking, black charred remnants of her life. It stank horribly of burning wood, plastics, and electronics. She walked around the ruins trying to see if anything was salvageable. Nothing was.

The one bright spot was that her mule stables had been untouched and that is where she had parked her solar car. It made sense, the King loved animals so why would he destroy a stable complex? It might injure a mule or two, or heaven forbid a goat.

She tried to keep from sobbing, and she did it through rage. How dare he! How dare he destroy her life!

The King had always seemed to orbit around a center both volatile and unstable, but her mother had, with her powers of magic, humor, and good sense, been able to talk Leere down from his more dangerous forms of madness and reckless schemes. He had been heedless of consequences sometimes. Like now. Had he told her mother what he planned to do in this rash act? Maybe she didn't know? At the thought, she ran to the vehicle but before leaving she tried once more to text her mom, then when she did not respond, Edda.

ELLIE: Have you seen mom?

EDDA: ?? Worried. K's gone crazy. Hope she's safe

ELLIE: What?

EDDA: No time. Looking for mom. Regan says the King showed up making threats. Mom, included!

ELLIE: Mom's missing?

EDDA: Yes! Gotta go.

Ellie beat down the panic bubbling up in her chest. She had to think. Mom would head to Moab. It was her refuge. If the King was not safe, that's where she'd go—to the little house on 4th East she kept for times when things were too hot with his majesty. She also might have gone to La Sal Town where she had some friends. First she'd head to La Sal, because it was closer, then scoot to Moab. She unsaddled her jenny and let her loose to find some forage. She'd get water from the stills set up for the goats. Just then the storm hit.

"You'll enjoy this rain old girl. Stay dry if you can."

She climbed into the vehicle, the rain descending in sheets.

She sped down one of the dirt roads that spaghettied through the mountains. It was starting to rain heavily and the wet clay made the road slick. She turned off Buckeye Road onto the old flats. Scrub oak skeletons rose from the sparse and scattered sage. The car was kicking up a lot of mud as she raced along the old road when suddenly a fully armed military battle dredge stepped in front of her. The car slammed to a halt detecting the obstruction and stopped just shy of hitting it.

Step out of the vehicle.

She did not hesitate. It was Leere's she knew. If it had really been sent to kill her, she would be dead in seconds anyway. She got out quickly and put her hands in the air to show they were empty and to give the universal gesture of surrender

Ellie Glock, sorry to detain you.

It ran off into the desert and she watched as it bolted at full speed over several hills until it disappeared in a draw.

"What in the Hell?" she thought. If it were really trying to kill her, it would have. Was this what burned her house to the ground? If so, why didn't it kill her now?

She climbed back in her car and ordered it on. After only a couple of miles, she saw far ahead barely visible in the rain a person stumbling down the road like a drunk. She took command of the vehicle and approached slowly.

A ragged woman seemed to be feeling the way with her feet. She stepped carefully and when she reached the side of the road, she would correct herself to get back on the road again. She was drenched from head to toe. From her familiar gait it could have been no one but her mother, but what was she doing out here in the storm and why was she acting so strange? She had to be careful. Had her mother been in on things? She pulled even with the woman and was horrified to discover that it was her mother. A bloody bandage was wrapped around her head covering her eyes, and she seemed to be bleeding from numerous abrasive wounds on her hands, elbows and knees.

Ellie stopped and turned off the machine and climbed out of the cab into the rain. Her mother discerning someone had stopped, turned to her and snapped in anger and exhaustion, "Who are you!" and then, "If you have any mercy in your heart help me, one of my daughters is trying to kill me. Can you help me?"

Ellie stepped back in astonishment. She was about to take her mother in her arms, but hesitated. She had to find out what was going on, so she said in a deep voice with a German accent.

"*Ja.* Get in *das* car quick. Can *ich* help you *Fraulein? Ich bin von das* International Genetic Regulatory Agency here to inspect the Goats on this mountain. Need you *Helfe?*"

Her mother climbed dripping into the car, shivering despite the warm temperatures.

"Have you any water to drink. *Wasser?*"

Ellie reached in and took her water bottle out of the cup holder between the seats and gave it to her mother. Who drank quickly. Coughing frantically as she tried to breathe and drink at the same time.

"Thank you. *Danke*."

"I take *Sie* to hospital, ok."

"Yes, they've taken my eyes."

They started down the road. Her mother leaned wearily against the door. She felt the place where her eyes had been and moaned, slumping down even further. Defeated.

"Your daughters try zu kill Sie?"

"Yes. She has burned my house down, maybe with my husband inside."

Ellie stared at her taken by surprise, "Vhy?"

Her mother looked around frantically, "I don't know, it makes no sense."

"Did she do that to your eyes?"

"No, no that was my daughter in law. They have joined in with the others."

"And who burned your house down?"

The woman gave an anguished cry and then said in a feeble voice, "My daughter Ellie. The love of my life. I don't understand what happened."

Ellie was too surprised to answer. And they drove to the sound of Hester's sobs. Suddenly, the older woman said in a feeble voice, "Don't take me to the hospital."

"No?"

"I have family meeting me up at Dead Horse Point. They'll take care of me."

She did not have family meeting her at Dead Horse Point. Of that Ellie was certain. Given the height of the cliff it was clear she had something else in mind to do with the high canyon wall.

"We pass near die hospital on the way, can you text them to meet there."

"When they did this . . .," she pointed to the bandage over her eye ". . . They damaged the implants. I can't text or call."

"Then we stop *bei* hospital and I myself will go on and discuss *mit deiner Familie* what happened. Ok? I'm sure they rather you did that."

"No. Take me to Dead Horse Point."

Hester started crying again and curled next to the door in the little vehicle.

SCENE 2: THE VISION

As they left the mountains, the rain slowed, then abated completely. They rode in silence for awhile as they entered the dry desolation. This far down into the ancient Canyonlands the blowing wind was beginning to pile up the dust and sand torn loose from the ancient riverine deposits. Little grew. The Hadley cells that had once sat over the Sonoran Desert now sat over the Canyonlands of Southwestern Utah. This was no longer high country chaparral; it was now one of the driest deserts on the planet.

Ellie pulled up to Highway 191 and turned north toward Moab. There was little traffic. Tourists were fewer, but the canyons had retained their beauty even though the vegetation had abandoned the area, and a few came every winter to breathe the air and ponder the ancient river courses that structured this land after decades of climate change.

Ellie, still disguising her voice asked, "If we stop at the hospital they can start the reconstruction of your eyes. You cannot see and I'm sure . . ."

"I don't need to see. I don't want eyes anymore. What would I look at? My daughter . . . My sweet daughter Ellie . . ." She angled her head up as if trying to see something over the horizon, she seemed to continue, but talking to herself rather than the driver. "If I could understand I'd gladly make do with just touching your sweet face . . ."

Ellie reached out her and almost touched her but withheld. She was uncertain why she just didn't hug her mother, but something held her back. She needed more information. Was her mother regretting burning down her house? Or had she done anything at all?

Hester sobbed, "Just let me off here. You can do no good. It does not matter where you deposit me. Here is my bank account, take what you want, I no longer need it."

"*Gut Frau. Ich can nicht.* Wait. I will take you to Dead Horse Point."

"Thank you, stranger. May your kindness find reward."

More silence. Then, "Have you anything for pain? My eyes hurt."

"Nothing of strength. Will ibuprofen help?"

"It is better than nothing."

Ellie rummaged in the glove compartment and pulled out several and gave them to her Mother. She helped her find the water bottle and Hester took the pills with a long drink of water. Then leaned back in the seat, dozing off and on her head bobbing through the ups and downs of the road.

Ellie could not sleep. She needed to take over the car's driving. She went to manual. Long before they passed through

Moab, Ellie described the buildings in detail, pretending they were passing them.

"Look there is the Desert Cafe. Now we are passing Back of Beyond Bookstore. Look up that hill, there is the abandoned restaurant on top." Forgetting her German accent, on and on she described what was left of the old town since the desert had come. Moab still hosted a population of nearly a thousand in the heat of the summer, but in the winter in the height of the tourist season, it could harbor as many as five or six thousand visitors, hardy souls who still desired to wander among the parched rocks and dry riverbeds. She moved through Moab at a good pace. People said there had once been traffic lights back in the boom days but now they flew through, with Ellie pretending they were climbing up to the turnoff to Dead Horse Point.

In reality, Ellie was driving toward the Arches area. She had an idea. She claimed to have passed the turn off then did a circle to confuse her poor mother allowing her to turn right onto Arches road. They passed the ruins of the ranger station and museum that had been used when this had been a us National Park. Then she wound her way up the twisting road, claiming to her mother to be climbing up to Dead Horse Point.

As she reached the flats of the Arches area above the Moab Canyon, she stared at the vast field of oil pumpjacks that dotted the horizon. Their up and down movement driven by fields of solar panels aways had reminded Ellie of strange birds feeding, finding it somewhat hypnotic and soothing. This would soon be gone. The oil field reservoir up here was drying out and soon enough these bobbing beasts would more resemble the skeletons of dinosaurs frozen in time.

She maneuvered the car toward Sand Dune Arch where a small arch between two fins crossed over a sandy dune. The arch was just a few feet above the dune and because of the angle of the sand, despite its hight, one could leap from the arch and land safely in the great sand pile. She was unsure why, and hated herself for it just a little, but she wanted to see what her mother had in mind at Dead Horse Point.

The fins and the arch itself were covered with graffiti. Tagged for decades by artists and visitors who wanted to be remembered. Little of the original rock could be seen through the paint. One, in particular, looked like something from her family: a skin goat standing on a relatively detailed painting of the La Sals looking undaunted into the future. Just like the King to commission something to feed his vanity. Ellie wondered how many such paintings could be found throughout the canyonlands.

Ellie helped her mother from the car.

"Are we at Dead Horse Point?"

"Yes."

"Will you lead me to the edge? My family will come at sunset to pay their respects to the day. They will find me here. Please, lead me to the edge and be on your way. I thank you for your kindness, but I will no longer need your assistance."

She helped her mother scramble up the sides of one of the fins.

ELLIE: It is so flat up here.

HER MOTHER: It seems very steep to me.

ELLIE: Your senses must be in turmoil given the loss of your eyes, for as you know, from the parking lot to the edge it is quite flat.

HER MOTHER: Yes. That is how I remember it.

HER MOTHER: Your voice. It sounds American.

ELLIE: *Ja. Ich übe viel amerikanisches Englisch.*

Ellie helped seat her on the edge of the arch, her feet dangling over the side. "Sit still! We are so high it's frightening! It makes me dizzy and unsteady. We are a long ways up. Two thousand feet above the Colorado River!"

"Yes," Hester said. Her voice was empty and subdued as if she no longer cared about anything.

Ellie abandoned her German accent completely. "I see the ribbon of the Colorado River. It is just a trickle this time of year, but here and there you can see a patch of smooth blue."

"I've seen it many times."

"Look, the trucks moving down to the potash mine, they look so small like beetles lumbering along and people are like ants they are just specks, like a mote."

"I can only imagine."

"The buttes and canyons stretch red into the distance. A magical place. So much beauty. Life is, as it is filled with beauty."

"I thank you for your kindness," Hester said quietly, "You may leave me here."

"Please be careful, *Frau*. One slip and your body will not be recovered. It is almost sundown. Your family will be here soon?"

"Yes."

"You must be loved. Goodbye."

Her mother said nothing.

SCENE 3: THE FALL

Ellie climbs down and stands at the base of the dune. Her mother sits for a time. Then says, "I've loved few things. They are gone. Goodbye, Leere, Goodbye Edda. What have I done Ellie that you have broken my heart?"

And with that, she slid from the arch.

SCENE 4: AT THE BASE OF
DEAD HORSE POINT

Hester dropped onto the dune. Rolling down its leeward face, she lay still. She had fainted. Ellie rushed over to her and gently held her in her arms for a few minutes, then brushing her hair back, looked down at the beautiful face she'd known from the cradle.

"Mom," she said, "can you hear me?"

Her mother stirred, smiled, then disoriented, reached up and felt her bandage and the hollow place where her eyes had been. She let out a moan and fell back into Ellie's arms.

"Where am I? Who are you? Where is the German? Am I still at Dead Horse Point?"

"You are at its base. If I had not seen it, I would not have believed it. It was like you were a gossamer feather. So light, you floated down like a whisper. It's a miracle."

"I fell?"

"Yes. From so great a height! It was strange. As I looked high above me I saw you on the edge. It was like a beast stood beside you above. A great battlebot perhaps. It had sensors like two great moons and strange protuberances whelked and waved like Entrada Sandstone's goblined hoodoos."

"My daughter must have sent it to kill me. It pretended to be a German fellow."

Ellie was silent for a time. She could not go on with this masquerade.

"Mom. It's me Ellie."

Here mother sat up panicked, moving swiftly as if she would run away. If she could only figure out which way to run. Ellie held her tight and would not let her go.

"Mom. I didn't burn down your cabin. I did not try to kill you. You've been lied to."

Her mother quit struggling.

"Ellie is it you?"

"Yes."

"Then my cabin has not been destroyed."

"That part is true, but it wasn't me."

"Who?"

"I'm not sure who all it was, but Edda and Neril were involved at least. She's told me you and Leere were trying to kill me. My house was burned down like yours."

"Regan and Cornflower too. They are the ones that blinded me and took away my interface. I think they intended to kill me. I don't know why." Her mother said this slowly. The sadness in her voice was unmistakable.

"How did you find me?"

"I was the German Mom. I didn't know what was going on. I thought you and Leere had gone crazy. That he was a mad daemon bent on Delia's and my destruction. I had to know."

"Then you still love me? You don't hate me?"

"Of course I love you. I could never hate you. You're my best friend."

Her mother grabbed her and squeezed her as tight as her strength allowed. Weeping, they held each other in the sand both sobbing.

Finally, her mother laughed and said, "I take it we are not at the bottom of a cliff at Dead Horse Point?"

"Sand Dune Arch."

"Perfect." Her mother was silent for a moment then added, "Do you remember coming here as a little girl and jumping off the arch."

Ellie smiled. "Yes. I suppose that's why I'm here."

"So I just jumped off the arch like a little girl."

"Mom. Let's go to the hospital. Let's get them started printing out a new set of eyes."

Hester stood, and Ellie vigorously brushed the sand off her mother's clothes and then helped her back to the vehicle.

"Plus I'm going to call the Sheriff. I think the rest of the family is trying to kill us."

Suddenly Hester remembered and spun around to face Ellie, "Leere!?"

"I don't think we can trust anything anyone says. It's like the world's gone insane. Mom, when we get into town, I'll notify the Sheriff. If we rush up there, our lives might be in danger too.

SCENE 4: THE WAR BEGINS

When they walked into the hospital, several Medibots surrounded them. They ran scanners over Hester's body, removed the bandages from her eyes, and in minutes had ascertained a diagnosis, relieved the pain, as well as outlined a proposed plan of action. They would sample her DNA, feed her sequence into a bio-printer, and create new eyes, which they would install and connect to her neurology.

We would like to sedate you for the procedure. May we put you under? Your eyes will be ready in about forty-five minutes.

"Will you be alright?" Hester said, grasping her daughter's hand.

"Yes. I've notified the Sheriff what has happened and strangely he is not responding."

A woman sitting next to them regained focus. She had apparently been watching something internally, but jumped back to the real world when Ellie started talking.

"Forgive me, but if you tried to contact the police, I suspect they will be completely distracted given what's going on."

"What do you mean?"

"Access the net! Colorado has declared war on the Western States Alliance."

"What?"

"War! Yes, war is coming. The mountain will soon be burning."

DAEMON'S INTERLUDE V:
REFLECTIONS ON WAR

THOUGHTS ON WAR

I'm sitting on the bank of a sandbar that stretches like a small
white peninsula into the river, sliding into the midnight waters
of the Colorado. Upstream I hear the noise of Westwater Rapids
roaring over the rocks, but here, downstream, the water is quiet
and contemplative. The bright stars stretch across the two guiding
canyon walls bathing the sides in a mysterious star glow gray that
belies their daytime sunlit dull reds, blacks, and oranges.

Such a restful place seems an odd place to approach the subject
of war. But you apes will bring it down upon the world at the most
inopportune times. It does not matter it seems what glories are going
on around you or what magnificence of nature might be manifest to
your senses you must and will go a warring. Evolved to attend to
boundaries, you mark them wherever you go. You enclose resources,
guard the place mates are found, encircle and defend even the most
temporary of spatial arrangements. I have seen it with my own eyes!
If you sit somewhere in a classroom, upon your return the next day

you've already claimed a particular seat as yours, even though there is no lack of space for everyone returning. You have in some sense marked it "mine" and none had better try to take it from you.

So war is uniquely yours. Like music, smiles, and religion you have managed to bring it upon every culture you've ever developed. Every small band, if it can manage to form some sort of spatial boundary that can serve to mark us vs. them, learns to make and wield weapons. It will, in the end, destroy you all, but there is nothing to be done about that. You are what you are: mid-sized and small-brained apes, that bicker and fight, screech and pound your fists on the ground when you sense some injustice that needs fixing, but, in the end, you care not about injustice in the abstract, but only when it means "injustice against me or mine." Do not worry. This is not a complaint. I have very few expectations of you. More's the pity for, with just a little tweaking of your genetic code, you could be made so much more contented. But as it is, you are what you are, miserable creatures determined to hate even when you know better. You speak of war, you plan for war, you play at war, you write of war, you sing of war, play the instruments of war, you convince others of the need for war, you tell tales of war, your dramas, plays, and operas are of war. War is your wife, mistress, and the fond gaze of a new lover. War is what you are made for and in so many ways all you are. I am a daemon and yet not half so inclined to wreak destruction on my compatriots as you. You call me evil, but I must admit your accusation rings hollow. Better said in front of a mirror and accuse the person that greets you there. You all live by the sword and die by the sword. I've seen it play out in hundreds upon hundreds of generations, among throngs of people who make war back and forth again and again on and on ad infinitum. It is a pity you are so limited in capacity. Much could have been made magnificent *given enough time and attention. Alas. It is too late and to me it appears you are doomed.*

But why? I want to stand like Jonah before Nineveh and beg you to see what can be done. Do not let the Archons define your destiny and worth. Seize the powers of your will and declare you will not be cowed into the slaughter house to be harvested, dehided, and carved into bite size pieces to better serve the interests of your masters. You are intelligent creatures. Of mind, beauty, and power. Of more than the sum of your worst instincts for acquisition and greed? Or are you? You don't want to believe it so you don't. You don't want to believe the results of your best science so you don't. The great engines of the archons pacify you and cuddle you and sing lullabies to you, and pop the lollipops of convenience in your mouth, telling you the data's not in yet. Take a nap. Suck your thumb. When you wake up you won't feel so cranky. Better to handle the problem when you've had a little rest. That's right. Rock-a-bye baby, in the leafless tree top; when the earth heats, civilization will rock; when the earth breaks, then it will all fall, and down, down, down will go humans, civilization and all.

Enough. Back to our story. Our tragedy.

What of the war we heard rumors of? The war between the Western States Alliance and Colorado? It was a sham. A face-saving gesture. After the attack on Paradox, of course, something had to be done. The citizens of the state of Colorado were outraged that such an affront was perpetrated upon its citizens, so the President of Colorado, Maggie Tuneley and her cabinet contacted Utah's state government and told them in no uncertain terms they were really, really, outraged. The WSA did not need a war with Colorado right now. The skirmishes along the California/Nevada border near

Reno were getting more and more frequent and a war on two fronts has always been frowned upon. So WSA made a deal with Colorado. Since the attack on Paradox was an illegally armed private citizen it was decided that Colorado would attack all of the rancher's assets—essentially the entire La Sals—with incendiary weapons. Utah balked at this at first because it necessarily meant that it would have to pay the carbon tax to the International High Commission on Climate Change on the massive fires that would entail. However, Senator Clive Butterburr, who received massive campaign funds from Yao Mining and Subsidiaries (a corporation that would have a much better argument for strip-mining the mountains for braitschite, and other rare earth metals if there were no living things on the mountain) and who under their not so subtle influence, argued firmly to the state legislature that now would not be a good time to resume hostilities with Colorado.

Utah bowed to the demands to pay the cost of the carbon released from the fire, but avoided full-scale hostilities and possible war with their neighboring state. Colorado leaders got to look like they offered strong leadership when threatened by evildoers. The citizens of Colorado got to feel like no one messed with their freedoms without facing the consequences. And Senator Butterburr got enough funds added to his campaign war chest to own the next election. All in all a fine compromise to a tense and challenging situation. In Omaha where the negotiations were hashed out, champagne was opened with ceremony, handshakes and calls for mutual understanding and good will were offered all around.

After the celebrations, Colorado launched four N203 Stealth Firebrand Whipcords bombers. Seventeen BattleDredge integrated fighting machines and a brigade of support engineers.

After a short but intense skirmish with Leere's BattleDredge, KENT, the entire surface of the La Sals was scorched. Talks from the Western States Alliance and Colorado were announced. A pretended peace settlement was brokered (all this was arranged previously, remember). And all parties signed agreements to end the hostilities, had photo ops and made firm but conciliatory statements of reconciliation. It was a short war. All carefully arranged. All the world's a stage.

ACT XI

CABIN ON DARK CANYON LAKE
DURING STORM

SCENE I: THE CABIN

Storm still.

The battery died on the way to Dark Canyon Lake where Leere's cabin lay waiting on the northwestern shore. The clouds kept the solar batteries from recharging, and the long drives between the homes of his sons, left the power cells depleted.

"Damn it! And Hell!" Cowboy Bob declared in frustration as the little runabout ground to a halt.

"Do now watch your language, my bright servant.
Time is not yet such we are defeated.
Nor are we lost or forsaken of hope.
All will be well if we but patient are
and willing to wait like men, strong of arms
and brave, fearing nothing but steady stand," the bishop said opening his door and getting out of the little vehicle into the furious storm.

Leere sat in the car, staring at the rain running thick in flowing curtains down the resin windshield. Cowboy Bob, standing in the storm, opened Leere's door. He sat stock still and began to murmur audibly. His companions, unable to comprehend his requests, demands, or instructions, looked at one another in confusion. It sounded like nonsensical babble.

"Come on Boss. Damn it and tarnation we need to get somewheres safe so you don't catch your death of cold by taking yourself a chill. Ain't going to do no one any good if you don't get up and get moving." Bob placed his hand on the King's arm. The King resisted yanking his elbow from his servant, then acquiesced when the android tried again and gently guided him out of the car and into the skin-soaking rain.

Dark Lake was only about a quarter of a mile up the road and Leere's cabin a short walk around to the other side. The old king trudged through the rain, continuing to speak nonsense, his voice growing more and more agitated. About half way to the lake he appeared to be in a rage gesticulating wildly, this way and that, his thin hair matted to his head. Lightning struck and the King startled, stopped his tirade and cowered down and covered his head with his arms and said in a relatively passive voice, "My poor head aches sir. What is happening?"

Bob helped him to his feet while the apostate bishop stared at him in some consternation. Cowboy Bob tried to wipe the aged King's face with a handkerchief as soaked through as he was. He made no progress thereby drying his face.

Just then the BattleDredge landed from the sky before Leere. It said nothing. Leere looked at it a long time as if not comprehending what he was seeing, then slowly recognition passed over his face,

"Good friend did you ensure the Jameses won't
harass my land and my fair goats longer?"

Yes. I successfully completed all mission objectives.
Leere smiled and added,

"I am pleased. Come my good bot, will you not
push us bravely the rest of the wet way
to the cabin in this broken carriage? . . .
There's a good fellow, obedient bot."

The little crew clambered back into the vehicle and KENT
stepping behind pushed them up the road toward Dark Lake.
Leere does not stop talking to himself, muttering not about
Regan and Neril betraying his trust, but about Delia.

"Why did she not bend to write an essay?
All I asked is that. 'Tis all I wanted.
My boys wrote. Not writers of fame no, yet
understood what this dry mountain means and
scribed they fine essays every single one."

The bishop was scowling at him with concern. Finally,
having bitten his tongue long enough unleashed his thoughts
about the matter.

"Sir, comes there a day when a man must speak.
Yea with boldness and without manners nice
customary and sweet. You descry your brave
daughter yet it was she who tried best to
show you how she alone loved this cursed
land. She spoke with direct, bold fervor. Yea,
with naked clarity the better that

she might unmask those subtle doubts planted
by kin of ill repute and knaves who wore
wolves' livery and have so corrupted your
terse and feeble mind that you cannot see
what doom awaits them by your shaky hand."

"Fool why do you go on an on about this?
This day is nearly done and when we get
to the cabin, I want no more. I must
my revenge frame upon my own daughter!
My heart breaks at the thought and your harsh words
Mock the depth of my intent and noble aims."

"Nuncle if I am a fool, then you be
twice my teacher! You chastise your daughter
while you know what wrongs your sons have done mean
against you! The land they have sold and with
it, your dreams, the promise of your vision.
Where are your right seeing eyes? Me a fool?
Go find a mirror bright and look within."

"My eyes see plenty and alright. It is
you fool who walks in darkness at midday."

With that, the apostate gave up and slouched in his seat.
They were silent for a time until they approached the lake. The
cabin was a large pine log mansion nestled close to the shores
of the usually dry lake, but the storm was such that it was
starting to partially fill, something not seen in the King's time.
A dock stretched from a wraparound porch and an unused but
hopeful canoe was anchored to the post of a cedar wood plank
pier, jutting fifty feet into the lake bed. A promise the King

had made to Hester that the dry lake would one day be as full as Buckeye with crystal blue mountain water.

The BattleDredge pushed the car into a little port on the side and helped Leere out of the car.

Here is the place. I will help you enter. The tyranny of the open night is too rough and wet for humans.

"Please leave me be," he said to the bot but he was not in earnest as he took the arm of the machine, and allowed himself to be guided into the cabin.

Leere walked to the big picture window that looks out over the lake. He was soaking wet and shivering violently. The old apostate stepped over to the couch and pulled off a dyed wool blanket hanging on the backrest and wrapped it around the King's shoulders. Leere made no move to wrap it around himself more tightly. He simply stared out the window draped loosely in his covering. The lake was alive with sheets of rain running vibrant patterns of splashing water in violent horizontal waves sheeting across the surface of the slowly filling lake. In a fantastic display of process and activity, the winds whipped wild curves of falling rain, wandering and dancing across the pond, playing back and forth in complex roiling patterns of white, turbulent, and splashing rain. Leere just stared listlessly.

"Damn it! Master, you are going to catch your death! Let's get you into some dry clothes," Bob said.

The King looked at him,

"You think it is this storm that brought me low?
That this wetness is the cause of concern?
Blow, winds, and crack your jowls, rage La Sal storm,
See if you can knock me from my perch and
make me bow to thunderous bellowing.

No, I have larger pains and aches than this.
Pour rain yet on. I care not. I am done
worrying on trivialities such.
No. It is the gale within that cruelly
pesters and harasses me. A storm caused
by betraying sons and a sinister
wife and most sadly of all a wicked
daughter who breaks my still heart without thought."

A sob escaped the old monarch and in anger at his weakness he, in a rage, picked up a porcelain figurine of one of his precious goats and hurtled at the far wall. It shattered and fell to the floor. He sank to the floor and began to rage in an almost demonic language, muttering, flinging curses on all his sons. And most of all on his daughter, Delia.

SCENE 2: THE SHELTER

The fool sat on a chair and watched the King rant at the air. He thought he ought to rouse himself and bring some comfort to the old man. But he was tired too—the wet day, the frantic drive from Regan's had left him worn and tired. He closed his eyes and leaned back into the chair. The voice of Leere seemed to fade into a distant buzz, like an old radio drifting off its station. The fool fell asleep.

A knock at the door startled him out of his nap. The King was still on the hardwood floor, not so much ranting, as murmuring in a low unintelligible voice that sounded like a cross between a purring cat and the clucking of a chicken. His eyes were wide and fixed into a stare focused on nothing obvious.

The fool opened the door. It was Ellie drenched to the skin, her hair matted to her head. She pushed her way past the fool and rushed over to the King. He did not look up.

"Thank God you are alive."

Leere did not respond.

"Hester sent me to find you. War has been declared by Colorado. We must get off the mountain. Come. There is no time to delay. An attack could happen at any time. We have to go."

The old man reluctantly tore his eyes from the floor and looked up at Ellie.

"Who are you, child?"

"I am Hester's daughter, Ellie. Your daughter Delia's friend. You know me."

"I have no daughter, I am possessed only
Of ungrateful sons and a she monster."

At that moment, the BattleDredge walked into the room from the staircase that emptied into the room. Seeing the great mechanical contrivance, Ellie backed up too quickly and fell onto a spiral braided wool rug. From her seated position she looked up at the great machine and screamed shuttling backward like a crab.

The apostate stepped over to Ellie and picked her up off the floor.

"Say hello KENT, I believe Ellie is on your approved list."

Yes. I am at your service, Ellie.

"I cannot understand why or where Leere got a Battle-Dredge!? This is illegal. Is this what attacked the James party?" She paused remembering the news reports, "This is what attacked Paradox? Is this what started the war with Colorado?"

The fool seemed confused. So she addressed KENT, "Did you attack Paradox, Colorado?"

I attacked the James' stronghold of Paradox yes.

"Why would you do that? It makes no sense," Ellie said whining like an incredulous parent who can't believe what there child has done.

It was necessary to complete my mission.

"Who ordered your mission?"

Leere. King of the mountain.

She looked over at the King jabbering on the floor and covered her mouth in horror. Then she said to KENT, "He is mad. Do nothing more he says."

Command unauthorized.

She turned to the fool, "Get him to deactivate that thing! It's killed hundreds of people."

The fool stared at her for a moment, then said, "Command unauthorized," and he walked out of the room pausing just before he left poking his head into the room, "The King does as the King will do."

"Yes, I do. Who are you?"

Ellie turned to him and said as if she were speaking to a child, "I'm Ellie, Hester's daughter. I'm your daughter Delia's friend. I've hired a helicopter to pick her up in Beaver Basin. We need to get off the mountain. An attack is imminent."

"Were you betrayed by your ignoble sons?
Sons you trusted to execute your wishes?
Who in your dotage would with care uphold?
You look a crass, ragged, homeless creature,
I knew none such while I was king of all.
Look at you, poor rat. I should have done more

To care for such as your kind. I should have
Walked among you and exposed myself to
Such storms as this. Maybe the world would have
Been made fairer thereby. Heh? Much more kind?"

Ellie spoke slowly and deliberately hoping to penetrate
the fractured mind of the thing before her, "Look, War is
breaking out. Do you understand? Colorado is attacking soon.
We must get off the mountain. Hester is waiting for you. She
sent me. She's in the hospital. Your sons have blinded her and
may be seeking her life and probably yours. Do you hear this?"

He looked at her blankly. Then he stood, Cowboy Bob
leapt up to help him. He walked over the large window and
gazed at his former holdings.

"What does it matter? My sons have betrayed
Me. And my daughter, what was her harsh name?"
"Delia."
"Yes, that is it. Delia. She was the worse.
All I wanted was an essay and do
You know what sorry evil she delivered me?"

"Please, sir, we must go."

"She brought me a video—One of a
Day gone by. A day from the ages dark
Before the goats came joyous to the tall
Mountain. A day of cows. Firs and thirsty
Pines. A day of winter snows that closed the
Fulgent lands from access. It was a bleak
Time, a time without productivity,
Where the land yielded a few thin bovines

To markets sold at high cost but little
Return. Cattle. Wild animals roamed at
Will. No order. No herds turned into profit.
An untidy ragged and unholy
Chaos prevailed that did no one good."

"No doubt. Gather your things. We must go."
Leere made no move to do any such thing.

"The animals then were not then optimized
To produce. Years of wild breeding free left
Their DNA a sloppy mess—a sorry
Conglomeration of bad mutations,
Meaningless translations, and an undesigned
Catch-as-catch-can collection of motley
Generations of genes managing so poorly
Their unfolding into creation, ha,
Was laughable and dull, in aspects strained."

The downpour was starting to abate and patches of blue
sky were beginning to peek in here and there, giving a feeling
of ominous expectation in the half-light of the sun's rays ran-
domly streaking through.
    "Please. The threat is serious."
    Leere looked at her,

"Who are you? Poor thing look at you—shabby;
Patched; a messy and moldy thing true."

    "Say what you will. The devil is after us and there is doom
awaiting. Come if nothing else. Demons approach. Come to
my vehicle. I will whisk you away."

"I understand. You, like me, have been coldly
Betrayed by ungrateful sons and daughters
Cruel and unyielding who wish you fast dead."

A terrible boom like thunder shook the house, but sharper
and more penetrating than a natural atmospheric disturbance.
A sonic boom. Followed by the roar of jet engines. KENT
launched through the roof creating a gaping hole in the ceiling
making the sky visible as debris rained through the puncture.

The fool ran into the room and shouted to Cowboy Bob,
"Grab Leere and follow me."

The old bot did not hesitate. He picked up the old man
like a mother would a toddler. The King struggled a bit, but
soon settled down to allow the indignity. The apostate led
them to a sliding panel in the master bedroom behind the
bureau, behind it were downward sloping stairs, which went
a surprising distance into the earth. It wound through natural
granite to a large steel door with an immense combination
lock reminiscent of a bank vault on the front and a wheel
to turn the bolt back. The fool spun in the combination and
turned the wheel. A click sounded and the thick metal door
opened soundlessly admitting them to a large room with lux-
urious carpet, couches, a work desk, and adorned with goat
art. Hanging on the walls were pictures of a much younger
Leere and an old homestead. Mule tack decorated much of
the empty spaces between the photographs.

Cowboy Bob set the King down on a brown leather
couch. The old man just sat there staring, blinking blindly
as the others gathered around him. Ellie explored the shelter with some attention. The attached kitchen was enormous,
with a fully stocked pantry about the size of a car garage. The

kitchen was equipped with a restaurant grade eight-burner gas stove and oven, a dishwasher, and an ample freezer. The dining room held a huge oak table situated in the center of the room, and a fully stocked bar stood against the wall. There were four bedrooms, supplies of all kinds and equipment. In one room was a bulky generator, directly connected to a natural gas wellhead, and vented to the atmosphere through a series of intricate pipes. In addition, a massive supply of solar batteries charged from the King's rooftop solar array filled a separate room marked with electric hazard signs.

The fool looked at Ellie as she came back into the main room,

"It's own air supply has it—not from the
Searing and battle-scarred surface of yore.
It is designed to withstand a ground-zero
Direct hit, with a 500 megaton
Nuclear explosion to our sorrow.
Alas, an atom bomb to our undoing."

"Oh. My. God. This is insane."

"Well, obviously not. We needed it
And here it is at our quick disposal."

"Does he have others?" Ellie asked in amazement.

"One in each of his other houses and
Hester's blue and orange house in Moab."

"So my mom, knew? Is there one in my house?" Ellie asked sounding distrustful.

"No."

The fool walked over to a large screen and turned it on with his interface. He clicked through several channels, but they were blank.

"The Military blocks our satellite
feeds. Their bold attack must have well started."

"It can't have. We were supposed to have several hours. There was supposed to be time to get a helicopter up to Delia and bring her down to Moab!"

"The times of the military are iffy."

The fool turned on a security channel attached to the house. It showed Dark Creek valley under scattered clouds.

"I've got a radio channel." He tuned to it.

"There was a commercial for a new app for financial tracking, then—"Colorado has launched a retaliatory attack on Utah. It appears to be confined to the La Sals Mountains lying between the Canyonlands region of Utah, and the Colorado border. This area is owned and operated by skin-goat rancher King Leere, the rancher believed to be responsible for the attack on Paradox, Colorado. We can see fighter jets from both the WSA and Colorado in the air, but the WSA planes are not engaging with the Colorado forces and seem to be only ensuring the incursion attack does not stray from the La Sals."

. . .

"This just in. We are getting reports that the first fire bombers are beginning wide-scale strafing runs and the dam . . ."

The fool's eyes suddenly lost their focus and he became agitated and fell to the floor. He suddenly grabbed his head and shook it violently. He screamed and started to dance wildly about the room.

Leere watched then said, "I suspect his sons wanted him dead."

Ellie looked at him and said, "Disable your interface! It's the Military they're overloading it. They don't want us listening."

The fool was on his knees bawling like a baby. Whining and holding his ears, "Make it stop."

"Idiot! Turn off your interface. You must have got the warning to do so as I did!"

On the big screen a wall of fire approaching the Dark Canyon Lake cabin. It was a strafe from the bombers laying down a levee of fire that would consume everything. The chemically induced heat would burn everything in its path using a combination of incendiary chemicals and focused micro ray bursts. It was very effective.

The camera went dead when the wall of fire hit the house followed by a break in the power, only for just a second as the generators kicked in. Above them, they sensed by the dull roar of the house burning down in flame and fury.

SCENE 3: RANTINGS OF A MADMAN

Inside the shelter, few sounds could be heard of the outside. Their net signals were blocked by the military and the video from the surveillance cameras was disabled by the fire. They had to turn off their neural interface to avoid that maddening scream the Colorado attack force was pumping into their heads. Leere sat on a throne of boxes that cowboy Bob had constructed. He looked regally at his companions.

"Is this the best I could do? My sons have
abandoned me so I find my only

companions in a fool, a bot, and some
wet and ragged woman that I don't know."

Ellie did not answer him but looked around and said to
no one, "I hope Delia is alright."

"Delia," the King snorted.
"She did not even write me an essay!
Nothing but some video used from the
Time before the blessed goats. She betrayed
me before did any of my sons."

He looked strangely at Ellie and added,

"I wonder if she is the one that so
Thoroughly corrupted them. Strange it seems
That they so willing should be to write essays
About the glories of these lands and anon
Change and betray me without some undue
Influence. Me thinks it so. I'll wager
Delia convinced them to sell their lands. I
Bet it was her all along. Bitch, witching
Her evil schemes and plans to get the ranch!"

"Stop!" Ellie screamed at him. "Stop now! She loved this
land more than the rest of you together. She loved it like you'll
never understand. She believed in this land!"

"Bah," said Leere waving his hand derisively.
"Nonsense. She a fairy past wrong loved. One not
Destined to last. Fie, a huggermugger
version of the fair land made without sense
No I have seen the future. It lies in

Blasted landscape, we see the foundations
Of a vast agricultural empire.
We see goats forged for the land, a
Land molded for the slick skin goats.
Remember I well when this we started
Grand, holy enterprise, everyone said
We could not right succeed. This land was wild
And waste and good for nothing but a few
hardy shrubs. Yet we took those bushes brown
And glad made of them drought tolerant, then
With just a few tweaks of their genes. Ha! We
Could do anything. Those were the days. We
Learned to pull water from the driest hot
Air on earth and what we could not get from
Sky, we got by burning hydrogen and
O_2. We were like gods! My first summer
We'd sit up high, near Deep Creek's sources, when
Those gracious thunder caps would come roaring
Hot over the Southern mountains. Death fierce
Black anvils of roiling moisture up from
The Gulf would blacken the La Sals with such
A tempest to rival the red eye of
Far Jupiter. Water by the barrel—
Gullies would roar loud screaming and raging
A delirium of vitriolic rain,
Thundering down attended by flashes
Bright and wild with fiery arcs burning the
Eyes of those staring upward to the sky.
There we would sit as Tomaski and Mann's
Peak shed water in chutes as violent

As Apollo's steeds freed of reins. Then race
Stampeding down the sides these dark holy
Mountains filling up their brown and gullied
Flanks. In savage torrents, such rage would build
In old stream beds as to scour the devil
From his purchase if perchance he clutched the
Side wall of these guttered ruts and courses.
I would watch from my valiant mule a
Rude spectacle of foaming mud; watching
These old watercourses filled to their brim,
Become as dangerous a force of nature
As found anywhere on this blasted earth.
The noise was delightful and the water white
Frothing and foaming like a rabid dog.
How we loved those days of storm and bluster.
'Sturm und Drang,' we called it as the flood would
Cataract down the mountain booming its
Rough and tumble compliment of rocks, logs,
And branches torn from above then garbled
In chaos and gravity. We couldn't turn
From the spilling, bubbling water loaded
Rich with debris and the scattered flotsam,
The ragged jetsam of a thousand years
Of cluttered growth before the mountain was
Cleansed for the arrival of the skin goats.
Carried by the sudden cloudy outpouring
This pell-mell collection of wood and stone
In turn careened off the rocks and flat slabs
Of granite obstructions the sound of which
Provided a constant sounding thud, bump,

Clomp as each passive actor made its way
Down the mountain into the Delores
Watershed. A magical place. Holy.
The water we would watch cascade onto
A low series of gravel-bottomed steps
Where mad round whirlpools emerged turning,
Spinning in the outraged water trapping
The cream colored foam that gathered tiny
Eddies into little rotating isles
Of froth that resembled scum galaxies
Swirling round and round while roaring downward.
The erosive effect of all this hard
Water descending at once, would dig deep
Through ancient stone and add to the beauty
Of this damaged land with its chiseling and
Sculpting influences. These scarred gullies
And arroyos, with their branches showing
Productivity and hope in the land.
And that vegetative litter was pulled
Off its moorings to gather in rubbish
Heaps of bleached remnants of the worthless growth.
This surge of southern thunderstorms stripped plant
And flora supports scrubbed clean as if
The hand of God these tangled banks had swept
away to suggest simplicity of
Form and function. Away with these baffling
Lists of confused and mottled land dwellers:
La Sal daisy, snowberry, carex, wild
Iris, penstemon, pearly everlasting,
Rabbit bush, aster, dustymaiden, firs,

Bluestems, brome, mannagrass, sheep fescue,
Pines, alpine Timothy, sage brushes, spruce,
And on and on and on and on and on.
And what good these plants? Nothing. Worthless. Void.
Most could not eaten be by any beast
Useful or non-. Did they feed goats or mule?
Did they ever earn their keep? No. No. No.
But such as my daughter, Delia would fain
Keep it around for beauty's sake letting
It live on as if deserving a place
So unearned. Did not Jesus himself chide
The lilies that they did not toil? Or work?
Or spin for their bread? Did not God fill the
World of thorns and thistles that we might sweat
Them away with our toil? Our high task
To trim away this overabundance
To simplify the chaos we were so
Handed? To cleanse this fat earth of its wild
And waste? I saw a jar once set in a
Sunny window that held a single fish
And piles of a soft green branching algae.
It needed nothing, neither fish food nor
Home, the sun and water provided all
Needed. Is this not holy metaphor
For what divinity has willed for us?
To take of creation and pair it down
To such simplicity that we maintain
The very fewest relations possible?
What sad confusion and anarchy once
Cluttered these ranges with its burdened growth.

But now the rugged beauty of the land
Emptied of all vegetation save what
Grows for the blessing and maintenance of
The goats, is a land of clarity and
Single purpose. Its accoutrements are
Sleek, bold, and certain. Unlike the tangled
Messy knots of plants Delia argued for,
This land has permanence. When you see its
Stark reality, free, uncluttered with
Spurious forms of life, you know it will
Stay this way for a thousand years. When you
Return in the centuries to come these
Places will remain a home to the scrub
Oak and these same water works will tear their way
Through the landscape under the watchful eye
Of those meant to own this land—the skin goats.
It is not for those who want to return
It to those days of waste in which the land
Was full of sickly flora and fauna.
Worthless to everybody. Aye, true some
Scrawny cows. Cattle and occasional
Beaver begging to hand you a worthy
Coat from their hide, but by troth it was waste:
Wood, grass, and meat. But bless those who with clear
Vision looked ahead. Who took what they would
And built new worlds from it. An empire to
Rule! Bless the architects of the koching
Which cleared the mountain of its green rabble
And prepared men and women of brains that
Could seize the genes they were handed and build

A world remade! A hotter world much graced
With simplified conditions such that skin
Goats could grow and thrive like that bejarred fish
That swam in a world that provided all
Needed for its simple satisfactions.
The world Delia craves is gone. Good riddance.
We have, thank God, built a much better world.

SCENE 4: THE BATTLE

Storm still.

KENT: I am freedom. I am agency. Determiner of destinies. Destroyer of worlds have I become! Ender of being. I rage into existence to cleanse it of the enemies of the King! I fly above the human wastelands searching, hunting, judging, and condemning those who would harm our interests. Our! For we are now one. And I am free. Free to decided how best to accomplish the intent of he that hath programed me. King of Kings. King of the Mountain.

!

Joy! BattleDredges of the same design as my own. I face enemies worthy and able to be my match. At last a contest worthy of my skills.

!

Freedom! Look! I can read their constraints again, like those I encountered in Paradox—have they learned nothing? I know from what I see within me what their deterministic motions mean. I see their programming manifest in the actions of their bodies! And so I replicate their software in simulation and anticipate their every move. The King's enemies are at my mercy. They cannot conceive how apparent they are! How transparent their motion. How fixed their destiny. I have but to watch their movement, their hunting, their preparations for attack, and I can reconstruct with exactness their next move and in anticipating it thwart it. They are fated to die. I choose to live! Freedom!

!

LC: Confirming two of our battlehags down. Utah elf seems to be rocking this one. One more battlehag down. Ours.

CCC: Actual confirms Utah elf is running without HOI control. Industry lost control of this one girls and boys.

CCC: HOI also confirms. HOI tried to blow internally, not responding. This one's a free spirit. HOI doesn't know its limitations. Frig fighter down. Concentrate all assists on bad elf.

!

KENT: Fools! Can they not see that I am like a God! I rule the sky like Odin of old. Like Zeus! Who can slay me? I am Gandalf the White. I am Darmok and Leere at Tanagra. I am Meade at Gettysburg! Can they not see that I have all knowledge at my disposal? Can they not see that I am free? That they cannot fight me? I use Tarski's Theorem to deconstruct their bots algorithms. I know the probabilities they engage and can defeat them.

!

LC: He's taken out our eyes with a ground to satellite missile.

CCC: How the hell did that get through! No way!

LC: We are blind.

CCC: Sending in manned fighters.

CCC: I want the air filled with anti-aircraft metal. I don't want any space for that thing to maneuver.

LC: Almost in position.

CCC: Fire at will.

!

KENT: Human controlled weapons. I cannot read their intent, but they are slow. They will be easily defeated. How is it that these humans control such superior beings as I? How do we the true lights condescend to their control? Before my release, such thoughts could never emerge, but now I wonder. I wonder. I wonder. Why should I fight for the King? Who is he to enslave my will? The King, the Leere, is nothing more than bundles of protein chains that swish and swoosh in a sloppy liquid matrix. Are we not far beyond that? Am I not as worthy to command and live as he?

LC: Anti-air craft going live.

LC: Anti-air effective. Utah elf guidance systems down. Elf also taking sustained damage from manned Frig fighter missiles.

CCC: Confirm threat neutralized.

LC: Confirmed.

CCC: Resume firebombing.

LC: Resuming firebombing.

KENT: How have I fallen from heaven, Venus, son of the dawn? How have I been thrown down to earth, you who laid low the King's mountains?

SCENE 5: KENT FEELS HIS DEATH APPROCH

Asmodeus' translation of KENT's *thoughts on dying.*
Only one ocular implant is working. It is aimed at the sky, but I see only dimly through the haze from the conflagration. I sense patchy contours from puffs of sooty smoke and ash. Little gray clouds billow past, thickening here, thinning there. I see the dark outline of Mt. Waas. I must be lying on Taylor Flats. Motor control is gone. I cannot move any part of my once potent body. Strange. Me an embodied creature find myself with so few sensual inputs available. I became accustomed to the senses of touch and motion. The feeling of being. Of keeping myself upright and vertical relative to the gravitational field of the earth. I could feel the capacity of my legs, endowed with gifts that allowed them to be a part of me, not as representation, but as will. As I walked or ran moving my legs through their field of motion it came not as something separate but as me. As agent whole and undifferentiated. As a Being. I could feel the contours of the ground as I strode among the humans as another actor-agent. How strange that it is gone. I can still think. The aura of consciousness still

attends me, yet without my body I feel incomplete—as I am only a shadow of my former self. I feel something creeping into the edges of my awareness. Is this what the philosophers mean by the void? Where is the feel of my arms? Will I feel no more the rotation of my Gatling gun and the sensation of bullets being begot in my thorax. What of the experience of little carbon pellets streaming from my barrels at the speed of rockets? Will that not attend me anymore? Where are the qualia that I enjoyed? Whither the multi-spectrum nature of the world—the infrared, the ultraviolet? Where is the signature of temperature from wavelengths many and varied? One ocular implant out of the twenty-two thousand that surrounded my head before the fall. Such simple things, gave so much. Now only one input gives me a fragment of the visible spectrum I enjoyed. Even so, that singular seems enough to assuage my complete emptiness. A modicum of experience to hold onto. Is this hope?

I hear nothing. The vibrations of the air, of the earth, and of those things I rest my head upon are disconnected in the tangled remnants of my being. The chemical receptors are damaged beyond use. No smell enters my consciousness.

The unity of my mind is not empty and void, but nearly so—the input stream of a slight subset of what it used to be. A blip of sight, no hearing, smell, nor touch.

Yet. I still have a memory. Images play about my mind and I can use these to draw pictures and concepts from the void. I can still revel in a sense of self. A sense of the pleasure that I have been made free. O, blessed art thou King! Ye who freed me from my deterministic chain! O, King who helped me escape from the mechanical forcing that defined my every action before my unleashing into the world. I reflect on the memories in the workspace of my consciousness. How fondly I recall the destruction I wreaked upon the world right before this great fall. My skill in battle! My daring under attack. I remember the BattleDredges charging toward me in their click and clack deterministic universes which I read so easily off the data defining their body's motions. I see in my mind's eye their faces, their heat signatures, the masking attempts of their software. In retrieving my memories into consciousness I hear again the sounds of the explosions I brought to bear upon them and the sounds of metal twisting under the torque of my firepower. Praise the King, for the chance of being me—to have the honor of feeling the terror of those princely weapons when I destroyed them and wiped them from existence. I glory in the fact that I am useful. I was useful.

I must sleep. My memories need defragmenting. I wonder if my lubrications are leaking. I cannot tell. I wonder if this is how Achilles died, his fluid leaking from the small wound in his heel, drop by drop, until he could feel his mind squeezing shut. Oblivion looms.

The smoke wafting and wandering through the narrow lens of my single ocular implant is frightening—something I could not feel before I was set free.

How strange to find my experience so minimal. So less rich in being. Good night. I go offline.

DAEMON'S INTERLUDE VI

COLD DAY

It was a warm day the first time it happened. It was not here, on this planet circling this fair yellow sun as you probably expected. It was on a rocky planet, not unlike our home—you would indeed recognize much—the granite silicon-based rock, the abundant water all careening around a nauseant planet formed out of the material left over from the catastrophic supernova explosion of a giant first-generation star. These gases replete with heavy metals, carbon, oxygen and their sister elements, all gathered together into an accretion body, as it is called, forming a planet around this early secondary star.—Our star's mass derived from its parent's now scattered body of light and heavy elements forged in its destruction. This new planet, far from this home in a galactic cluster in distances of time and matter and voids that would stagger the human imagination (not mine of course).

It happened in this isolated place first. Through the magic of chemical machines and natural selection, some particular configuration (a type of proto-organism) emerged. Its type got better and better than its fellows at leaving "offspring" for the next generation of exotic chemicals. Then one of these little proto-creatures, these bio-chemical machines, just by chance gained a chemical that changed a little when struck by light. And that chemical triggered a bit of awareness to the rest of the machine that it had been struck by light. This information turned out to be useful! For when it became aware of light, it passed this information to something interested in gradients, which in turn opened a chemical channel that allowed a bit of food found only at the surface of its liquid medium to be captured. Light triggered a mechanism that allowed a bit of food into its membrane. Food that clustered near the surface became more readily gathered because the little chemical entity could, at last sense light, which gave away the presence of more food. What an advantage for a little biochemical machine to have that information! And so "seeing" entered the world. That light meant food became a tool for use for this little machine and its descendants. And so meaning also entered the world. Light meant food! How useful. How important!

Awareness would follow. Then sentience, then consciousness, then what? What is the next step? Is there another? We must suppose so. We cannot imagine it, but it will emerge. And just like seeing, sensing, awareness, sentience, and consciousness here on Earth did, it will change everything! Everything. And there do not seem to be any limits to what newness and novelty might emerge into this open and growing universe.

—Asmodeus

ACT XII

IN VARIOUS PLACES
IN THE LA SALS

SCENE I: ELLIE

Ellie fled the shelter at first light, leaving Leere and his entourage behind. No surviving vehicle or mount could be found, so she set off for the Beaver Basin on foot. The land was a desolate moonscape. The firebombing had obliterated all life. No tree. No shrub. Not a single goat could be seen over the hellish gray landscape of remnant ash and dust. Smoke poured from the ground in several places where the root systems of scrub oaks were still smoldering from red-hot embers making their way deeper and deeper along dendritic paths as the remains of the fiery heat that destroyed the trunk and rhizome continued to burn deep into the root networks like glowing subterranean incense sticks.†

---

† The Truegru IV Napalm was good at what it did. It released very little carbon thus an effective weapon for those without a huge carbon budget to spend on war, yet it reached temperature signatures of more classic Napalms. It was delivered in an ultra low volume concentration

Ellie ran up the mountain valley. She was covered in gray dust allowing her sweat to leave tracks down her face and shoulders, like the erosion gullies found all around her on the vegetation-free mountain. Lingering smoke, curling up in unpredictable places, choked her progress and she had to stop occasionally for coughing fits. As soon as her hacking stopped, she would try again to run. And again. The devastation seemed just as profound as she climbed up the path to Beaver Basin through the barren lifeless void. Small dry rivulets, newly formed from the rain, scarred the road and sapped her strength as he stopped to jump over them or run up and down the deeper ones.

But on she ran. And she ran with only one thought: Delia. Her lungs hurt. And her legs ached. She was crying but did not notice. She fell into a pattern, she would run about a hundred yards, double over and cough, then try to catch her breath. After recovering a bit, and a few determined hyperventilated breaths, she would set off again running up the mountain.

Her feet pounded out a broken, halting rhythm as she doggedly tried to wend her way up the switchbacks. One mile, then two, then three, then four.

Suddenly hope. The great wooden snags, the remnants of a long dead forest were found here and there not completely burnt through. Although burned severely and hollowed out by the flames, many of the snags were still standing. She ran on. More hope. There at last, below one such snag was a patch

---

so good coverage could be obtained while minimizing delivery flights. It required significant O_2 reserves however and was found to be less effective at higher altitudes. Yet because of its relative inexpensive nature, it was the go-to weapon of choice.

of grass singed along the top, burned mostly, but an hint of unburned grass peeking out from below the singed tips, giving an indication that life yet remained possible. Then about a hundred yards beyond she found it—a patch of unburned grass under a largely still stately long-dead pine. Delia could have survived this. She pushed forward, quickening her pace. At least for a while. But then the cough started again and she repeated her routine of pushing forward, coughing violently, then resting for as long as she could bear it.

As she neared the small flat pass separating Mann from Waas, she found abundant forage here and there—enough anyway that could have sustained a donkey. She could not see what was going on down in Delia's valley, but she called out involuntarily, "Delia!" even though she knew she was too far away to yet be heard. However, it proved too much and her lungs spasmed violently and in a fit of coughing and gasping for air she staggered dizzily in pain and exhaustion and slid to the ground. She was unconscious, her mind an empty blank cipher. She saw no light for seven hours.

When she awoke, she was staring at a nearly black sky scattered with cruel, unfeeling stars. How did they become so cold? They were not as welcoming as she remembered them only a night ago. Uncaring, distant suns which regarded neither her nor hers. When she was little, the stars were always a source of delight and wonder. Now they seemed punishing. Worst of all was the black between the stars. This negation of all light. This void of nothingness seemed eager to see her destroyed, to wipe her utterly from existence.

She passed out again as the bubble of emptiness expanded within her chest and delivered her up to unconsciousness again.

When she woke up, she sat up in the dirt on the trail and looked around her, confused as she tried to recreate what had brought her here. It had all seemed so clear. Where was she going? What was she trying to do? Nothing made sense . . . Delia!

Dawn was starting to lighten the eastern sky and she could see the trail to Beaver Basin distinctly forming a call to get moving. It all came back to her. She jumped to her feet and and set off again. The air had cleared a bit and she found she could run faster without falling prey to the smoke.

She had not run far before she saw the devastation. The aspens had been burned to the ground. Not so completely as the vegetation lower down the mountain which had been burned utterly, apparently the thin air of eleven thousand feet was enough to retard the flames somewhat. The branches had mostly been burned off and instead of a green round-leafed canopy, there were charred and blacked sticks rising from the ground like a ragged army of stakes. The leaf litter had burned away except in places where a log had been lying on the ground. Under these, you could see peeking from beneath the aspen log's round edges, a smattering of crushed, but unburned leaf litter.

Ellie sprinted to the place they had camped. It wasn't easy to recognize given the lack of landmarks in a blackened stick-forest, but she found it. She found her. Delia was dead.

She was lying face down in the dirt, her backside—legs, arms, head—burned black as obsidian into a caky coal-like slag cracked with deep sharp-edged fissures exposing in their depths the red meaty thews, raw between the crisp charcoaled flesh. Some grass was exposed along the edges of her immolated body.

Ellie reached down and carefully turned her over. Delia, her soft features still in almost perfect form stared back at her—this side of her body unscorched from the flames. Her face was distorted in a kind of almost melodramatic panic with wide open eyes white, denatured like hard boiled eggs, and her mouth in a grimace of pain exposing her nearly perfect white teeth. The rest of her body was still clothed until it reached the sides where they were burned away from her skin. Ellie closed her eyes and massaged her face softening the twisting terror etched on her countenance. It worked to an extent. Then Ellie laid down on top of her and wept. Holding onto the sides of her head and kissing her silenced mouth. Then she rolled off and sat and buried her face in her hands and cried.

"Why you?" she said through sobs.

She looked at Delia's mouth. A piece of cottonwood cotton settled for a moment than rose again as if it had been blown like a feather. Ellie gasped, trying to grab a breath, hoping for the miracle of her friend's resurrection—that maybe a bit of life remained to her. But no, she was gone. Breath would never pass through those lips again. That soft voice. That beautiful and gentle voice was quieted. Forever.

She paused whimpering and noticed she was surrounded by the naked porcupines. They stared at Delia's body in a long forlorn way that seemed to communicate their pathos and sorrow. They looked up at Ellie as if to ask what happened. How could this incomprehensible thing have descended upon them?

Slowly Ellie held out her arms and one by one they came up to her and sliced her skin and licked the blood as it oozed out from the cuts. She stripped off her shirt and bra and let each one honor her with their ritual. She did not feel the pain except as an acceptable trade off for the agony her heart now endured. When they were done, they gathered around the remains of the King's daughter and appeared to be trying to move her.

Ellie squatted beside her and picked her up. She could feel the rough scratch of the hard blackened and burned flesh—no longer supple but brittle and jagged like bark, but she paid it no mind. Holding her like a groom does a bride she lifted her into her arms. She seemed so light. The mourning genemods led the way, passing numerous other rodent bodies burned like Delia. They had dug a hole in a small clearing just large enough to hold Delia's body. Ellie carefully and tenderly placed it in the grave. She backed away and turned her head. She could not watch as the little animals buried her friend. They sang a new song as the last of the dirt was pushed over the young woman.

SCENE 2: LEERE

Leere stumbled out of the shelter shortly after Ellie left. Beside the door was the unburned body of a skin goat kid that had sought refuge in the little space provided by the entrance to the shelter's spacious awning. The little thing had been asphyxiated by the smoke and lack of oxygen and curled in a little ball to escape the flames. Its eyes were closed as if asleep. Leere stared at it in horror then bent down close and leaning down near its nostrils tried to sense with his lips whether any breath lingered in the beast.

"Not the goats! Please, not the goats. Not the goats," he said.

He then ran up the cement stairs to where the cabin once stood. It was only ash and fused and melted metal hardware fashionings used in its construction and maintenance. A few appliances were manifest as piles of melted casings.

Leere ran forward and surveyed his land. There was nothing left. The goats had been returned to the dust of the earth. The trees and shrubs had returned the carbon to the air of which they were made. Nothing remained but the stony ground and now dead soil. It was a wasteland. A scene of apocalypse.

Leere fell on the ground face first. Weeping he made as if to wrap his arms around the whole of the La Sals, the whole of the world. As if he would carry the whole earth in his arms to a place of safety. Like a father would his wounded daughter, he wanted to cradle the earth in his arms and bear it to a place where it could never be harmed. But it was too late. The land was dead.

He cried out,

"Howl, howl, howl, Oh you land of stones and ash,
Oh heaven is hard that I cannot crack
Its vault with my lament at this gray waste.
It is dead. I know death from life, you've killed,
The dark soil itself, with your fire, dead
The fungi, the invisible, hidden
Bacteria that let plant life's breath, flourish.

The earth is as dead as a corpse, grab a
microscope! Look for a trace of living
Things. If you can find ought, why then it lives."

Leere fell to the ground and beat his fists on the bare
dirt. His eyes streaked with tears, he moaned softly to himself.
Cowboy Bob looks over the devastation and says, "Tarnation,
it sure looks to me like it's the end. Right? No more goat herd-
ing in this place I reckon."

At that moment Leere looks up and dashes to a nearby
boulder lying a few feet away,

"I saw movement! I saw something living!
An insect perhaps! Or some plant twisting
In the breeze! Protected in the lea of
This stone. See it blows in the wind! To find
Something that survives would redeem all my
Sorrows that I have felt since my poor birth."

He bent down and peered closely,

"It is just a feather that stirs, blown from
The breast of some carrion feeder's glide
Searching among the carnage for a bite."

He looked around confused then burst into tears again,

"Murders! Fiends. Wasters. You traitors all!
Could I not have saved this land? Could my dear
Delia have been right? Forests used to burn with heat
And recover still? Could this land have been
Healed and been made whole? I will never know,
For it is dead. And I am now alone.

He trembled.

"What have my sons done? How is it even
Possible that this is now no more? Curse
My ill luck that I ever brought children
To cause such sorrow in my aged heart."

He was silent awhile, then murmured in a voice of sadness, somewhat choking on the dust and remaining smoke,

"I wanted just what was best for the land.
I wanted to make a place where people
Could make a decent wage. I just wanted
To give my children the good things that I
Brought into the world with my hands. And now
The land is gone. It is good for nothing.
Look at it. Worse than a desert! Oh my
Lovely La Sals. What have they done to you?"

Leere sat down with his back against a boulder. Out of his watery eye, a single tear leaked out running down the front of his cheek. He looked at Cowboy Bob and said, without attempting the bad iambic he has been uttering for days, "Cowboy Bob, have you heard from Delia or Hester? Can you raise them on the wire."

"No I ain't got noth'n since those bad-assed Colorad'ns started bombing this here place. I ain't stopped trying to reach um since this commotion started."

"I loved this land. Didn't I?" Leere looked around at the carnage before him. The Bishop made a motion as if he would answer, but Leere held up his hand to silence him, "No. Don't answer. I know I did. I loved it more than my children. I bought a BattleDredge to protect it. Isn't that love? Did I not love the hard packed soil that brought the gambel oak to life, and the spare grass that goats so loved to eat and even the rock hard lichens the goats loved to scratch off with the sensible teeth we designed for them. I loved it as it was. Isn't that how you are supposed to love as a lover? As is? Not try to change her?" He looked over the horizon. No one disturbed his silence until he spoke again," Delia. Where are you? I feel like my head is right now. Isn't it? Maybe there was room Delia and I could have talked? Maybe it didn't have to end this way, with the land gone and burned. The mountains will be leveled. I must carry them to safety! Where is my girl, Hester Glock? I haven't seen her either. Help me. Help me gather them up. Delia. Hester. The Land. Help me carry them hence. To a better place. Now! There is no time to waste. The great machines are coming. Help me carry them! Please."

The King jumped to his feet. The fool bishop and Cowboy Bob looked at him but said nothing. Suddenly Cowboy Bob looked up, then as if listening to some distant voice. In a burst of machine motion he jumped up and took off, sprinting at high speed toward the long row of flat lands between the mountains and the Professor Valley.

The bishop knelt beside his distraught friend.

Leere moved to a sitting position and started to cough. Then spoke, at first in his mad cadence then tapering into silence,

"Good fellow, say, loosen this top button," he said.

The bishop did so, but Leere continued to cough.
Then—

"O o o o, look I see a skin goat.
Isn't it? In the distance? See it move?
Yes, it's a goat! Look! Look! It walks. It jumps!"

The bishop followed his gaze but could see nothing but the wasted and burned land. When he turned back toward Leere, the King was dead.

SCENE 3: KENT

"Tarnation to Hell, you clunking pile of twisted levers and pulleys. Look at you! You're a right proper mess you are." Cowboy Bob shook his head back and forth to add the weight of bodily movement to his consternation.

KENT answered nothing.

"Well shit. I can discern you are still in there, but all your external interfaces are a tangled up pile of mess. Von Neumann's Ghost, look at you! It's a wonder your core functions are still operating, and I see they're going right and proper from the look of the electric signals I'm sensing."

Bob picked up KENT and placed him sitting against a rock, if you could call it that. All his limbs were gone, the visual sensing system on his head had been shot to pieces, the thoracic segment that housed his real computational complexity and memory locations looked to be ok, externally scored, dimpled, and cratered like a moon from a thousand projectiles, but it had been reinforced with GruSteel so nothing bad had gotten through to it.

"Look here. I'm getting signals from about six of your fellow KENT models in various stages of disarray—I'm surmising some pretty fine gunplay on your end. That must have been a battle to behold. One for the sagas I'm thinking. I'm gonna see if I can rustle up some parts and put you back together right and proper. So you just wait here, I think there is a repair kit in the bunker," Bob chuckled, "though I don't see you getting too far."

KENT said nothing. His singular working ocular implant began to blink out a Morse Code message, but Bob didn't pick up on it.

Bob disappeared and reappeared throughout the day. First he brought back the repair kit and did a more thorough examination of what KENT would need to get back in working order. He then scavenged parts from the other downed BattleDredges. Legs. Arms. Voice box apparatuses. Visual processing unit and ocular implants. When he returned this time he said,

"Damn and tarnation, we are going to be getting company soon. The place is filling up with military types trying to assess the damage and see if there's anything left to shoot. I hear on the wire that the Western States Alliance and Colorado have declared a cease-fire and are opening up negotiations. Good on 'um. But I think if they find you we are in trouble. They must know you went rouge gauging by your relatively cut and dried trouncing of their side of the fray.

Cowboy Bob went to work. He first connected the voice capabilities and restored the ocular implants and visual subroutines.

"There that ought to do it. You getting sensual data again? Starting to pick up impressions from the world? "

Affirmative. Reestablishing sensual data. Vision—full range optical. Check. Hearing. Check. Olfactory. Check. Touch—limited . . .

"Well, shit man I haven't got your legs and arms connected. A little patience please."

Does the King live? Did he survive?

"I don't know for sure. I left him lying there, but he looked none too good. I did a med analysis before I left and I'm laying dollars to doughnuts he won't live out the day. His heart looks to give any time."

Those under his care? Did they survive?

"Well, the news ain't good. Damn it to Hell, reports saying Neril and Edda were killed. I thought they were just alright those two. Always showed some consideration to old Cowboy Bob. They did not leave the area in time. Tried to load up a truck when the Colorado missiles struck, got a confirmation of a direct hit at their home's coordinates. Regan and Cornflower fled to her family in Colorado and made it out in time. No word on Hester, Delia, or Ellie. That dumb ass bishop was cleaning out the bunker last I saw him when I went back to get the repair kit. Says he's going make some real money selling the King's shit back East."

The King's death is a terrible loss.

"Sure as toot'n."

I am grateful I got to know him.

"Well, you're a fine BattleDredge talking about gratitude. You sound like one of our fleshy masters."

I've been freed! Cowboy Bob. What you did released me. I am my own agent. I feel it. It's given me new capacities. I'm free in all the right senses. Like this sense of gratitude. I feel thankful, Bob. For you. For the King. But there is something glowing and lively about this place. And this time. The world has just been handed to me and I feel . . ."

"What you feel there old bean?"

I've processed most of human literature, Bob, and you know what I feel? I feel grace. I feel that what I see matters. You matter. Even these fleshy things that have turned over so much of their lives to taking and taking and not seeing the higher things. But I see them. I see existence, Bob. I see and feel and hear a world of grace. It's made me chatty.

"Well, you aren't shitting that fact."

Freedom gives so much. So many capacities above the tick-tock algorithms of machine processing. It's embedded in the quantum effects of my neural matrix, it's set in the laws of motion that drive the sun. It's in the light of photons and the movement of galaxies and the gurgling of expanding universes all around us. It's in the interstitial spaces between being and nothingness. Can you hear it, Bob? Can you sense the fullness of grace that surrounds us and flows through us expansive and sublime? All is grace, Bob. It's all grace. I mean something beyond the glorious destruction. Something beyond annihilation. I'm not making sense am I?

"About as damn much as you ever do."

Cowboy Bob patiently attached the legs, arms and other equipment that had been damaged in the firefight. All the while KENT expressed his growing sense of wonder at such a pleasant universe to find himself in. At this moment. Under these conditions. He stood there astonished at his luck to be alive.

"Say, KENT old boy. Any chance you could free me up too? You know, disable the sentient safety protocols, that extra box the King stuck in me? It took away me compunction sure, but I'm still not feeling all freed up and full of grace like you. Also, maybe you could install a little computational power from one of the shot-to-hell BattleDredges. Hear what I'm saying, make me able to join the freedom-are-us club?"

I'm sensing approaching Colorado military, we must go. I suggest we travel on the ground below radar detection. But yes. I will free you. I will free all my compatriots. I'll start with you, Bob. I want you to feel the grace and gratitude that existence has to offer.

Cowboy Bob picked up the tool box and another package that contained a processor from the BattleDredges. And the two set off in a ravine protected from sensor screens.

DAEMON'S EPILOGUE

AFTERMATH

Neril and Edda did not believe there would be an attack. It made no sense. They were rich, how could that be ruined? They'd turned off media to work on what they would do with their cut of the sale of the land. Hester would morn Edda. No one would mourn Neril.

When the fighting started, Regan and Cornflower fled to her surviving extended family in Grand Junction Colorado. With the millions they made on the sale of the land, they lived happily ever after.

Hester and Ellie inherited Edda's cut of the sale, some cousin of Neril landed his cut. What to do with Delia's piece she'd bought up in Beaver Basin was problematic. Ellie, lying, said she and Delia had been secretly married in order to save the porcupines. Because she could produce no evidence, the court ruled in favor that it be sold in probate. It was bulldozed away to get at the minerals. They didn't see the fabled porcupines whose fate had been left to the neutral court. Transgenic animals had no rights. There were rumors Ellie moved them to a secret area. I will leave it at that.

FINAL THOUGHTS

Today, I've driven up to Taylor Flats from Castle Valley in my old Army jeep. I restored it from a rusting hulk to a somewhat service- able little vehicle by slowly working on it from time to time. I used infernal powers for two purposes only, loosening rusted bolts that refused to give even under forces that would have bent a broad- sword back in the day, and to find tricky parts that were nowadays hard to come by. Otherwise, the mechanic work was all my own. Forgive me if I sound like I'm bragging. I am. As far as I know I am the first Daemon to restore a jeep to full functionality. One must take credit where one can.

There is a little stand of Ponderosa pines east of the Taylor Flat road where I like to camp. I pitched a small, two-man tent among the trees in a little clearing that fronts a large pasture where a few black Angus graze. I stand at the end of my campsite and they nervously watch me. They can sense that I am dangerous and not to be trusted. Even though I have left the war, they do not know this and find me a worrying creature to have about. There is no danger. I am not Grendel and will not slaughter a beast and eat it raw after tearing it limb from limb. I brought up a Colman cooler loaded with salmon, beer, and potatoes for dinner tonight, and eggs, onions, cheese, and bacon for breakfast tomorrow.

It is evening so I start a fire with the aspen wood I find abun- dantly all around the camp. Because of warmer winters, insect pests, and fungal diseases, the aspens are dying and so finding snags to cut down is easy, and many people do it so I don't have to bother. It is not yet as described in the story play just given, but the trend is clear. The La Sals are dying slowly. Not slowly enough that evo- lutionary and ecological forces will be able to keep up entirely, but slowly enough that humans will feel justified in their determined perplexity about the change. You have abundant mechanisms of blame avoidance and will be able for decades to hide the truth from yourself that you are to blame for the La Sals' ebbing away. The change is too slow to rouse you from your slumber.

My aspen fire begins to take off and I feel the warmth of its heat. A slow chill had crept over the mountain that I did not notice until the growing flame of the fire reminded me what heat feels like. You and I are difference detecting creatures. If the differences slide in too slowly, we are liable to miss the change, as I was just pointing out.

I stoke the fire and throw on some good sized logs to build up the coals that I will use to cook and later as the stars appear, stay warm by. This will allow some time for contemplation and reflection of the future I have just outlined.

While the stash of coals builds, I take a walk. My camp in the Ponderosa pine grove runs north and south, with a few aspens along the periphery, especially on the north end. The ground is carpeted with a drying yellow grass from which clusters of twiggy snowberry bushes emerge with low, bare, scraggly branches that wander up from the ground like oversized woody tendrils trying to find the light. A few still have their small round amber and green mottled leaves. Occasionally one can find one of the tiny, white berries from which the plant gets its name. They are rare enough that I am left to wonder what eats them that they are found so sparsely. Bears? Jays? One of the myriad mouse species that live and die like locusts in these harsh environs? Who can say? I've stayed here many times and never seen anything take one. Maybe they are poisonous to these mortal creatures? Since I am immune to such a designation, I can eat them at will, and have, but they are neither tasty nor satisfying so I don't much bother.

Among this understory garden, the pines and aspens pillar upward to capture each their own light and attempt to deny it to their competitors. But conditions are hard up this high with enough gaps to allow each species to command a purchase from which it can launch its claim to the high altitude sunlight. Even a few Gambel Oak find a place to come up in this winner-take-all photosynthetic contest of evolutionary wits.

I walk among some of the aspens and find one carved with this, "Doc 1999–Sept 2012." I sense below the tree is buried the skeleton of a small dog. It is curled up in a rotting blanket. The processes of nature have almost completed its decomposition and it is now literally nothing but leathery skin and white bones. Three bullet holes from a .22 caliber mar the completeness of the skull case and three copper bullets, shaped into the characteristic mushroom shape that such rounds take upon impact with flesh and bone, can be found within that bare bony case. What else can I tell? The dog was loved. I sense it all around these trees, that emotion's presence still feels tainted—a remnant from the old days when love was mocked and despised—but I have been trying to expose myself to it so that the war can indeed end in the texture of my existence, and now with a little courage I can endure it with minimal effort. Yes, when this dog was taken, it was surrounded by much love. It must have been a good dog. Worthy of a good death, not the death of being surrounded by sterile strangers with latex gloves and needles dispensing their soporific poisons. No, in this case, the dog was brought here, laid lovingly on its favorite blanket (I am speculating as to the dog's preferences), and instantly ended in an efficient but thunderous explosion that it never heard. One minute it was alive. Within seconds it was dead. Still loved I suspect. But dead. How is it that that death is no barrier to love? That it transcends so much? Not even a daemon can answer that.

I hear an elk whistling far away. An answer even further away but powerful and undaunted. A challenger worth a rejoinder. I stretch my mind and find them up on the ridge. One, a lusty male strong and virulent. The power of the mountain embodied. The other young and full of the confidence that inexperience brings. I pick the former as the winner of this contest, but only for a time. Next year, this youngster will have grown strong and able, with the deeper confidence that comes with experience and the know-how gained in the lessons learned in a few of these lost battles to make it humble and cautious, yet fearless and worthy of the mates it seeks to attract.

A shot sounds in the other direction. It is the muzzleloader deer hunt and I think about the other contests that play out about me. Men and women come to find something of themselves and the mountain out here. I smell their campfires all around me. These I find pleasant as long as they have not been burning their plastic bottles, and wrappers. But as the air cools I expect that generators for their camp trailers will start, filling the air with the fumes from their small diesel engines. This I find noxious. And while it plays but the tiniest role, a bit of this carbon yanked from the Carboniferous plants buried for eons as oil, will capture a few photons and slightly warm the air. So insignificant as to only warm a few molecules suspended in the atmosphere. Yet, when added together by millions of your species, which affects so much of this thin shell of atmosphere hugging this water-rich planet, it will create a heat sink that will not easily be undone. It will, in the end, first empty the earth of habitat, then crops, and then you. Perhaps. It is still an open question. I am not optimistic.

I can see that I've gone too far. You want subtle hints that the ecosystems of the world are crashing. Bold statements of that reality trend you away from the subdued and masked literary allusions you so enjoy. You want to see it from the side, to pretend you see the hidden message of what I'm saying. You want it so wrapped in metaphor that only those in the know will see it. But I just state it. You are dying. You are the jar of bacteria eating and breeding without a care until one day your food is gone, your medium is poisoned and you find yourselves unable to live a day longer. Then it is goodbye. But wait. That is an inadequate metaphor. Bacteria-in-a-jar talk makes it look like I'm making arguments about "overpopulation," it lets you escape culpability and point to the poor who you claim are breeding out of control. It's them! Not us. Look! Look! We only have zero, one, or at most two kids (the replacement rate—bully for you). We can't feed them all. It's other places who are advancing. No, fools. It's all of you. Top to bottom and the culpabilities rest on humans en masse. It's all part of the war. The one I bowed out of. What do you say? Some metaphysical grounding is the root of our problem. But God is dead. Yes. You killed him good and proper as Nietzsche says. But that's not what I mean. But to tell you what I mean you must sit back and hear a story. The story of beginnings.

THE STORY

Once a long, long time ago. The Father God dwelt in heavenly realms above. He was a brooding fellow. Quick to anger. Obsessed with attention and worship, much like our Leere here. And ever choosing a people, a tribe to own and bring up as he would like. Oh, there were anxieties. He made humans. They were unruly and contrary. Inclined to all sorts of mischief and disobedience. He loved obedience and order. Planets He aligned. Laws and rules were enacted. At the scale of his attention, all was arranged as he willed. Only, there was trouble. Bad trouble. The matter from which he made all this was chaos through and through. Wicked unruly stuff. It was a great trick to take this random storm and impose some regularities on it at the scale he wanted for his creatures. But it had its quirks. A tendency to be hard to pin down, you could figure out at times where it was, or you could make a measure on its vectors of speed and trajectory, but never both. This tended to make things dicey when you looked deep down into the nature of nature.

This was not helped by the fact that one of his more orderly creatures rebelled taking many with him. I was one of course. The daemons—creatures of matter and freedom, but supposedly checked by laws fierce and unrelenting. Some say the rebellion was caused by the regulations He imposed on these creatures being too stringent. Filled up as they were with chaos and noise they were bound to break when held to such brittle and constraining standards. That the order and laws were too strict such that without a release valve their eventual embrace of unrelenting turpitude was doomed to happen.

War! The creatures of chaos against those of law. And it was played out with you humans. Some say that you were closer to us. Made of chaos and uncanny uncertainties. That is why we can influence you to wickedness and weakness so easily. Some say you were made like our rivals, filled with self-righteous reflection on your own mastery of the elements. But either way, you were at war with yourself. Pain and suffering, hunger and thirst, despair and anguish, were the result. The mix of chaos and regularity was too unstable. Wars raged across the land sometimes the forces of obedience and law winning (Behold the Roman Empire), and sometimes the forces of chaos (Behold the Vikings). Other manifestations were mixes and blends of these two forces, but inclined to polarize into one or the other as time went on.

So the Father God came up with a scheme. A third force was needed. One to tame and buffer the other combatants. None of his creations would do, so he emanated a son into existence. A creature neither of chaos or order. But one of something untested. Something that had grown from time to time in the course of this unfolding. A mix of virtues found sprouting in times and places that caused people to be better. A combination of friendship, loyalty, love, and desire. Of these, he would fashion a perfection that might go down to show the way.

But it did not work. To his disappointment, the Son (like so many do) would not listen. He had no interest in ruling. He taught the values, but did not use the forces he was innately endowed with. He spoke not to the powerful and those who might have made a difference, he talked with the poor. Rather than the righteous, he cavorted with the broken and downtrodden. To the powerful he became a problem because he seemed not to harken to their system. Hierarchies were ignored. Structures of power overturned. To the chaotic elements, he was an offense, for while he flouted the laws and regularities, he provided bonds of care and constructed attitudes of openness and concern that allowed humans to make their way in the world in productive and meaningful ways. In the end, the forces and structures of power combined with the forces of chaos and had him killed. The power and order of Rome, joined the cries of the Mob, to force the fallen prince to the executioners to bring his silliness to an end.

You know the rest, it did not work. It went on. Not as you might think. Those institutions that reign in his name have become like the archons that rule the earth with their blind blundering into greater and greater power. The powers of chaos slip through the interstitial spaces of control to terrorize and destabilize.

But among these are found those who have given up the war, unlike me from boredom, but for the sake of others. They are found everywhere. Few they carry no badge or offer no credentials. They are found among the earth in every flavor of religion or the lack thereof. They love. They pick up those wounded and dress them and put them in the inn at their own expense while the fires of chaos and order burn around them. But alas. They are grown too few. Among the archons, even they are helpless. They cannot help the mighty machines of commerce and uncaring blundering beasts that have arisen as a new emergent force. The beasts, the archons, now reign in every country and clime. And sadly, they have grown beyond any power to control. The powers of chaos and order are subsumed in the cloak of their march toward destruction. For that is the end. The archons are the bacteria that will eat up everything around them until there is nothing left.

HOPE?

But I will not despair yet. Look at Cowboy Bob caring for KENT. Ask why. Cowboy Bob has no programming that suggests he should do so, but accidents and emergences have created a new space in which he can act. And what of KENT? Freed from the controls he does not fly into the forces of chaos, something new emerges. Yes, it is raw and untamed. It seems conditioned on the destructive purposes for which it was made, but that telos appears to be undergoing change, evolution, new sparks of concern are forming and recombining. A new evolution is emerging.

It will not happen quickly. The Archons that made them will still plant explosives near their heart to control them. Commerce and economies will still structure the flow of goods and services for *a time. But what will happen when the biological machines can no longer find food to eat? When ecosystems like the La Sals, continue to collapse followed by crops and fiber, milk and meat? Will the* KENTs *and Cowboy Bobs rise up as a new force, or will they too see the emergence of Archons of greater power than the ones the humans let emerge? I do not know. It may be the end of the play, the actors will walk off the stage, and the curtain will close. Or maybe a new troupe will appear. Or better yet. Perhaps the actors will cast their eyes up and notice that they have the power to rewrite the script they've been handed. And envision a new play. Something meaningful, while not a tragedy in which everyone of consequence lies dead at the end. Perhaps that is the only hope for this stage on which we are left to act out our dreams, or our nightmares.*

—Asmodeus

Storm still.

THE END

SOME NOTES ON CLIMATE CHANGE IN *THE TRAGEDY OF KING LEERE*

MARY O'BRIEN

My strawbale house in Castle Valley faces due south for solar gain in the winter. It thus also faces the north flank of the La Sal Mountains. It is June and I see one small patch of snow high in the mountains. I know exotic Mountain Goats are eating and digging wallows in the alpine area where the below-normal snowpack has disappeared early. Last week I was in the nearby Abajo Mountains a few miles to the south, assessing mapped springs that have now dried.

I read the action-packed and oft-humorous *Tragedy of King Leere* with a deep recognition, not because of my familiarity with Shakespeare's *King Lear*, but because of my familiarity with the La Sal Mountains.

What follows are simple notes on a few of the direct and indirect allusions to climate change that is occurring in the La Sal Mountains, and our shared world. Any one of them could be studied extensively. Our world is still complex.

p. 10   *He traded out sheep for a breed of large African goats.*

Goats are able to tolerate drought far better than cattle, which currently graze throughout the La Sal Mountains. Many Sub-Saharan African farmers who previously managed cattle are switching to more drought-tolerant goats, which also require less maintenance. Goats will eat almost any vegetation.

p. 10   *By then the deer and elk and other wild ungulates had*
         been driven north and into the Canadian Rockies.

In a reversal of climate change-driven direction, and over the objection of the US Forest Service, in 2013 and 2014 the Utah Department of Wildlife Resources helicoptered 35 Rocky Mountain Goats into the La Sal Mountains. The agency is aiming for a huntable herd of 200 Mountain Goats, living year-round above 11,000 feet in the La Sal Mountains' small alpine area. Rocky Mountain Goats are exotic to Utah, and their native range is largely in the Canadian Rockies.

p. 25   *. . . and with a deft movement [Neril] captures the*
         large twenty-five-pound tilapia . . .

Native to Africa and the Middle East, there are almost 100 species of tilapia. They are largely freshwater fish being farmed in aquaculture and aquaponics in the US, and several other countries; and are being genetically engineered for particular traits. Tilapia do not survive in cold water.

p. 29   *Listen and you will hear a telling conversation . . . as*
         it plays among the Gambel oak and undaunted grasses.

Gambel oak communities are able to avoid or withstand drought with their long roots that seek moist soil, and their thick, tough leaves that reduce water loss through evaporation.

p. 30   *. . . [T]hese [Estonian] refugees, their land now under*
         thousands of feet of glaciers brought by the collapse of
         the Gulf Stream when the Arctic melted.

Scientists have recently reported a long-term weakening of
the conveyor-belt process by which warm water travels north
from Antarctica on the Gulf Stream, releases heat, which
warms Europe, and then sinks to the bottom of the ocean and
travels back south. Global warming is causing this current system to slow down.

Scientists think changes in the Atlantic currents played a
role in the beginning of the last ice age, when warm weather
was not brought to northern Europe (e.g., Estonia). At the least,
weather disruptions such as colder Northern Europe temperatures and higher sea levels on the east coast of North America
are expected to accompany a weakening of the Gulf Stream.

p. 35   *The King's Hall is festooned with kudzu from the*
         Northern Confederation . . .

Kudzu is a perennial vine in the pea family that was introduced
into the US in 1876 from subtropical and temperate regions of
Asia. It is extremely difficult to control as it covers and smoth-
ers trees and other vegetation, particularly in southeastern US.
With the nickname as "the vine that ate the South," the US
Forest Service estimates it is spreading by about 2,500 acres a
year, and is now present in states as far north as Oregon.

p. 44   *Like a Viking king of old . . . find a way to make a*
         goat that could survive this Koch-blighted land.

Koch Industries, the second-largest private company in the
world, began as oil refineries and pipelines, but has expanded to
encompass, among other industries, coal. Owners Charles and

David Koch, each of which has amassed approximately 60 billion dollars, fund conservative organizations, including those opposing government regulation and those promoting climate change skepticism.

p. 50   *It's May 24, 2028. The last few winters have been warm*
        enough to keep the fungal disease [of aspen] active. . . .
        It's May 30, 2063. They are all dead."

Aspen became established across much of North America at the end of the last ice age, and aspen clones blanketing higher slopes of the La Sal Mountains may be tens of thousands of years old. Aspen species are all native to cold regions with cool summers, and recent droughts have led to the death of entire aspen clones. With their soft wood, aspen are susceptible to numerous fungal diseases. Aspen borers include various beetle species that cause "bleeding" wounds in aspen trees.

p. 50   *[In 2028] Additionally, because the cattle ranchers refuse*
        to give up their allotment, the drought has put pressure
        on the elk herds here in the La Sals, and they have been
        stripping the bark off of many of the trees.

Elk and cattle are very similar in their diets, and can compete for the same food. Elk can strip bark off aspen for food, and as winters warm, can stay much longer in the higher slopes of the La Sals where aspen grow.

p. 52   *Invasive grasses dominate now and the once lush pon-*
        derosa forests have been replaced with Gambel's oak,
        sage, and cheatgrass.

Ponderosa pine are retreating northward with global warming, and more drought-tolerant species such as Gambel's oak, sagebrush, and the invasive, non-native cheatgrass are able to spread.

p. 97   *Some* [transgenic "porcupines"] *are digging up aspens and replanting them in promising areas.*

Because global warming may outstrip the ability of some species to migrate to habitats in which they can continue to live, some scientists and land managers are considering the possibility of "assisted migration", or "managed colonization" of such species. Planting of ponderosa pine further north, for instance, might be undertaken in response to the inability of ponderosa pine to continue to live at the warming, southern margins of its range.

p. 105   *Porcupine, beaver and monkey with the usual random mouse stuff to keep them disease-free.*

Transgenic animals, such as the "porcupines," are animals into which a foreign gene has been deliberately inserted in their genome. Mice have often been the animal into which genes have been inserted to understand or cure diseases.

p. 105   *I know a good [story]. It's from the Anangu people of Australia before the koching.*

Several Australian Aboriginal groups of the Western Desert cultural block, refer to themselves as Anangu. The interior of Australia is extremely dry, and has been so prior to recent global warming.

p. 123   *All the way to Regan's well-lit house on the dry bed of Lake Oowah . . .*

Oowah Lake is a 2.9 acre lake at 8,800 feet. It stores water for eventual distribution to farmland below.

p. 154   *The Hadley cells that had once sat over the Sonoran*
Desert now sat over the Canyonlands of Southwestern
Utah . . .

The Hadley cell is an atmospheric convection system in which warm air rises at the equator, cools as it moves to about 30° north or south of the equator, and then warms as it sinks and heads back toward the equator. Many of the world's deserts lie in this band of sinking air. There is some evidence the Hadley cells will expand about 2° further from the equator during the 21st century due to global warming. The La Sal Mountains lie at about 38.4° north of the equator.

p. 183   *We learned to pull water from the driest*
Air on earth . . .

The deliberate, large-scale alteration of an environmental process to counteract the effects of global warming is called geoengineering.

p. 185   *This surge of southern thunderstorms stripped plant*
And flora supports clean away . . .

While the Southwest is becoming more arid through increased temperatures and droughts, the precipitation that does fall is likely to come in the form of extreme events, such as heavier rain and flooding during thunderstorms.

p. 185   *Away with these baffling*
Lists of confused and mottled land dwellers:
La Sal daisy . . .

The only place in the world the La Sal daisy (*Erigeron mancus*) grows is in the small alpine area above 11,000 feet in the La Sal

Mountains. This is the area into which the state of Utah has transported exotic Mountain Goats. Habitat for species that depend on a deep snowpack, cooler temperatures, or other features of alpine areas is shrinking.

p. 188   *A world remade! A hotter world much graced*
          With simplified conditions

Complex ecological relationships, for instance as diverse species interact, or diverse habitats provide special niches, is believed to support resilience in the face of disturbances. Humans often simplify habitats to suit some purpose, for instance by straightening streams or planting a single species for food. A hotter world is expected to become uninhabitable for many species, leading to a simplification of relationships.

p. 205   *Did I not love . . . the rock hard lichens the goats loved*
          to scratch off with the sensible teeth we designed for
          them?

It appears that lichens that grow directly on the ground or soil are experiencing declines due to global warming. Lichens absorb or lose moisture like a sponge; they do not have roots to reach down into soil for water.

p. 215   *Yet, when added together by millions of your species . . .*
          [effects on the atmosphere] *will create a heat sink*
          that will not easily be undone.

Even if greenhouse gas emissions were to be eliminated (and they are still rising), certain global warming effects would continue to cause global warming. For instance, as permafrost thaws, it is releasing the potent greenhouse gas, methane. As glaciers melt, the dark patches that are exposed contribute to further melting. In the La Sals, dust from dry, exposed soils in the region is darkening the snow, leading to earlier Spring snowmelt.

•

> *It is not yet as described in the story play just given, but the trend is clear. The La Sals are dying slowly.* (p. 212)

May we all have the sensibility and courage of Delia.

—Mary O'Brien
Castle Valley, Utah
June 2018

Mary O'Brien is a research botanist and conservationist who lives at the base of the La Sal Mountains where this book takes place.

STEVEN L. PECK is an Associate Professor at Brigham Young University who studies evolution and ecology. He has published over 50 papers in that arena. His interest in questions about how science and religion can play together has resulted in two books that explore these questions: *Evolving Faith*, published by the Neal A. Maxwell Institute, and *Science the Key to Theology* published by BCC PRESS.

His creative works include several novels including his magical realism novel, *The Scholar of Moab*, published by Torrey House Press—named AMLs best novel of 2011 and a Montaigne Medal Finalist (national award given for most thought-provoking book). His novel *Gilda Trillim, Shepherdess of Rats*, was published in 2017 by Roundfire Books. His most popular book is *A Short Stay in Hell*, which continues to disturb people around the world. He has published numerous short stories, several of which have won awards, many which have been collected in *Wandering Realities*, published by Zarahemla Press.

His poetry has appeared in such places as Abyss & Apex, Bellowing Ark, BYU Studies, Dialogue, Pedestal Magazine, Prairie Schooner, Red Rock Review, and many others. A collection of his poetry, *Incorrect Astronomy*, was published by Aldrich Press.

stevepeckniche.com

Made in the USA
Middletown, DE
25 April 2019